I0669080

Among
Animals 2

Among Animals 2

The Lives of Animals and Humans in
Contemporary Short Fiction

Ashland
Creek
Press

Among Animals 2:

The Lives of Animals and Humans in

Contemporary Short Fiction

Edited by John Yunker

Published by Ashland Creek Press

Ashland, Oregon

www.ashlandcreekpress.com

© 2016 Ashland Creek Press

All rights reserved. No part of this book may be reproduced or transmitted, in any form or by any means, without written permission of the publisher.

ISBN 978-1-61822-045-5

Library of Congress Control Number: 2016903383

Printed in the United States of America on acid-free paper.

All paper products used to create this book are Sustainable Forestry Initiative (SFI) Certified Sourcing.

Contents

Introduction

As I WRITE THIS INTRODUCTION, my hometown of Ashland, Oregon, is embroiled in a battle over deer.

Ashland is located on the edge of a national forest; it is not unusual for bears and mountain lions to wander through town. And over the past decade, a number of deer have decided that life among our homes is preferable to the life up in the hills. I'd say they're onto something. While the hills have suffered from drought and man-made thinning for forest fire mitigation, the lawns in town remain lush and the vegetation plenty, and the only current predators are the cars the deer must navigate among.

An increasingly vocal number of residents view the animals as a nuisance. There is talk of *culling* (a popular euphemism for *killing*). The words *vermin* and *pests* and *predators* have become common in newspaper op-eds and in city council meetings.

The black-tailed doe featured on this cover is one of our Ashland deer—and one of the reasons we settled in this town; we appreciated the fact that humans and wildlife coexisted here so peacefully. This new conflict between humans and wildlife is not unique to Ashland, however, and not unique to deer. Coyotes, mountain lions, bears, and wolves have all been labeled nuisances in towns across the country and even around the world.

These labels have played a role in determining which animals we hunt versus which animals we protect. But just as words can separate us from animals, words can also unite us.

I'm particularly proud of the words that come together within this second volume of *Among Animals*. This collection takes up where the first collection leaves off, introducing us to new species and worlds beyond our own. In this volume, you'll encounter dogs and cats, chickens and rabbits, a mythical bear, a kangaroo, a harbor seal, a mule, and even a cockroach.

As our society comes to terms with a darker future for the world's animals, it is not surprising to see many of these stories grappling with what this future might look like. In "A Sterile Place," a man near the end of his life reflects on a world that has lost a great deal of its animal life, including the frogs he'd loved as a boy.

In "Bight, Tomcat, and the Moon," the future is both dystopian and fantastic, viewed through the eyes of a young survivor on a mission to save her finned friends:

> *Moon's as full as she'll get since the Big Ebb—just a fish-scale sliver—since humans went walking all over her face in their fat white boots, then probes to study her plumes. Enough's enough, so she cut her ties and drifted, taking the sea with her. My father, a fisherman, caught the last of the sea, scooped her up, fish and all, into the Seahouse. "Stick to the roads," he said, "steer clear of ghost currents." So now I'm the moon to my finny friends, the tidal pull of my tiny sea until I find the true blue.*

As with the first edition, extinction emerges a bit too close for comfort. In "The Truth of Ten Thousand Things," we witness a ceremony marking the sad death of the world's last polar bear.

As we look at animals not so much as aggregate species

but as individuals, we can see parallels with our own lives. In "Strays," a woman's efforts to save feral cats mirrors the struggles she faces in her own life. And in "How to Identify Birds in the Wild," a bird researcher suffers from the migration pattern of someone she'd hoped to hold close.

In Australia, it's the kangaroos, not the deer, who are commonly viewed as pests. And in "Roo," Sascha Morrell writes about the messy aftermath of one such killing:

> *The thing lay sideways. It was the coat of the thing that first struck me—the soft depth of its ply, and colors in the fur like the memory of bushfires. Besides the blood. The tail was splayed.*
>
> *He wasn't yet dead. But we were prepared for that. I was brave enough to stand there while he looked back us. For a moment I even thought his eyes were fixed on mine, proud and soundless and affirmative. We were prepared for that. We were so fixed at first on his eyes and the red wound in his neck with its trickle of blood that it took us a moment to notice his pouch.*
>
> *Her pouch.*

And in "Shooting a Mule," technology and brutality merge into photographic history, reminding us of the sins of our ancestors.

Some of these stories explore animal captivity for profit and for power. In "Exotic Animal Alert: Please Post Widely," a retired circus trainer meets his match. And in "Phoenix Cross," the chicken industry is portrayed from the inside, from the eyes of a young man who inherits the pressures and the cruelty of running a chicken farm.

We share the animal kingdom with insects, who are all too often not seen as animals. Apart from bees, they are usually viewed as annoyances rather than vital contributors to our ecosystem. In "Vivarium," a woman comes face-to-face with a "monstrous, hideous" cockroach, with a surprising and hopeful outcome.

In "Lost Pets," wayward dogs become more than rewards for the narrator; they become the reward itself:

> Every time I pass a lost-pet poster on my street or in the park, I let a wave of pity roll through my body and then I keep walking. I'm like anybody else: I glance at the poster, I frown, but I don't for a second consider looking for the animal. I know better.

Children have a special ability to see things that adults do not (or are no longer able to see), particularly when it comes to animals. In "Julia and the Sea Bear," a young girl sees the past and future of a bear trapped on the beach between the cliffs and the ocean. And in "A Normal Rabbit," it is the children who see through the subtle abuse of animal competitions.

In "It Won't Be Long Now," a harbor seal strands himself in a woman's marshy backyard, leading the woman to step outside not only the safety of her home but the safety of herself:

> She wanted to say she was sorry—about the fishing line, about the flies, about everything—but he did not want her sympathy.
> "Suit yourself," she said. It's what she got for trying to help. She should just leave him alone and go back to the house, but some instinct would not let her leave his side. He was stranded, just like her. She was a bit seal-shaped herself, with almost the same number of chins. They were both full-blooded mammals, distant cousins, for better or worse. Here was a species who used to live on land but had decided against it. For some reason, the seals had chosen to go back to the sea. She wondered

if they regretted that decision, now that the water was
getting as dangerous for the seal as the land was for
Rowan.

Finally, in "Captivity," a teenager who feels trapped tries to set free a deer from a petting zoo—but in doing so ends up only further dooming them both.

Some of these stories are challenging to read. Others will offer hope. Taken as a whole, I feel that these stories point the way forward—to a world in which humans and animals coexist far more harmoniously than they do today. Animals have given their lives for thousands of years in support of human evolution. It is time that we humans return the favor by evolving a bit as well.

It is our hope that this collection not only open eyes and hearts, but open new ways of thinking and talking about our relationships with animals.

—John Yunker

Roo

Sascha Morrell

RICK'S REMEMBERING. "I heard once about a pair of feet that washed up on a Canadian beach. No body, just two feet in sneakers. No one could identify the feet. No one claimed the sneakers, either."

We laugh. "Two right feet, as I remember it," says Dave. His eyes are empty. We laugh again.

There seems no reason to be telling the story here, as far away from the sea as you can get without hitting the desert. But then, this did all used to be the sea, before the millennia made it the longest, driest beach in all the world.

Dave swigs, topping up his drunkenness.

The daylight is trying to save itself in a sinking streak on the far horizon, but above us the sky is night, already starred. Looking around the fire at the three faces lit from below, I get that eerie feeling I always get when I'm boarding a plane, surveying my fellow passengers. *So these are the last faces I'm going to see before I die.* But they say flying is safer than driving. Safer than drinking. I swig and Rick swigs and Dave swigs and tosses his bottle away into the clinking dark. Caleb sits rocklike, just holding the neck of his bottle, and in the glancing firelight I can't tell if it's full or empty.

...

It was good to get away without a word—without the moment in the driveway with the cuddles and the kissy canary noises and the promises to phone her every day. Turning onto the Great Western Highway with a full tank, bearing with the traffic then escaping it, leaving the city behind like some overflowing Ithaca to this space beyond space where the measures of the 600-square-foot apartment and the quarter-acre block are made laughable by a distance defying all Odyssey.

When I turned onto the dirt road, engine overheating and fuel light aglow, I no longer felt fugitive. I was now next to nothing. At the ragged seams of the distance, the lines of fences were still dimly visible, faint traces of ownership and law on properties the size of tectonic plates. And still driving on. Rick's is the last bit of freehold on this parallel: Any further west and it's all crown land on pastoral lease.

The last sign I saw on the road bore just one word, and that one hand-painted. HATCHERY. It pointed off at an angle into worthless scrub. Rick's drive was not signposted, but I knew it, even after three years. I knew its deadpan, level stare, its promise of fear. The gate stood wide open.

Beyond it, little had changed. Fistfuls of grass as dry as paper money scattered the crazed and shaven acres. Unknown tracks scribbled like snakes toward their crypts below the scrub. To the far left: the vast jaws of the bush. Crypts full of eggs and hissed whispers.

The creek was no more than a dry, broken spine. The gums hunched as if they were trying to shelter in their own shadows from the sun. One currawong gargled the air, defying the dry with liquid song.

...

"You can't fool us, mate. I know when I'm looking at a man whose soul's been strip-mined by a woman."

I swig. "Leave it alone, Rick. She's all right. She's good for me."

"Good for you. Hear that, boys? The wife's good for him."

I swig and toss my bottle back, hear it skiffling in the litter 'til it clips against another. Something else scuttles, back there in the dark.

There were twenty-three missed calls before I drove out of range—who knows how many more lost since in the ether. She'll have given up calling by now though. And of course, she'll have seen the note. I wonder briefly how she's taking it, what she's doing. This will be her third night on her own, and when I try to imagine it I just see her sitting there at her laptop—sitting alone and hating me and waiting for me all the same. Fingers hammering hard on the keys as she reworks that wreck of a novel: Penelope jabbing violent stitches into her tapestry.

At home, it's always a bit of an act. Pretending to understand her, pretending to know a lot more than I know, pretending to have read books I haven't read. I dropped the act, driving away. But I forgot that out here I have to put on the other act. Pretending to know a little less. Keeping the arts degree out of my voice.

The day's heat hasn't departed yet, and the fire seems needless. I have to grab another beer to water my headache.

It's a hard ache. We spent the whole hot afternoon shooting in honor of Stuart. Killing for him, or at least making loud noises about the killing we would do when it came our way. But the rabbits must have smelled us coming. They kept out of sight, or kept their distance, and we might as well have been firing air rifles. Caleb knew it—he kept his mouth shut and never fired a shot, but the rest of us weren't as smart. We wanted action. We wanted to shoot things dead in the name of our dead friend. I guess that's why Dave shot the kangaroo.

Leaving the Land Rover behind, we'd been walking a long while, heat strobing the backs of our necks, our backs drenched, my borrowed rifle heavy in my hands or on my shoulder.

"I say we try again tomorrow," Caleb intoned, but we didn't listen.

"This goes on much longer, we'll pack it in," Rick said. A bit apologetic—after all, it's his place; it was his invite.

Dave said, "This goes on much longer, I'll have to shoot one of you blokes."

Rick chuckled. "Well, in all this space, I reckon no one can hear you scream." And he looks at me. So does Dave.

"What you looking at *me* for?"

"It's not my fault you've got a head like a clay pigeon," Rick ribbed.

And we were talking and laughing as we trod the distance out on the scant grass, as we trod dried cowpats that crumbled like dark macaroons, and I had a big ripping grin on my face, thinking how easy it would be for us to kill each other out here, grinning because that made me feel alive—like I would always be alive. The homestead was way back behind us now when we looked: small and glaring the brightest white, its tin roof shelving light. Dry gums strained out of the land like screws of cork. Ahead of us the flat-packed paddocks ran on and on.

We strode and talked—talking about Stuart, his widow and kids and the good old days before wife and child, and we talked about women, and Dave told again about that rifle range up in Queensland Stuart had showed him. I thought about the Stuart only I knew, at university, but said nothing. We talked about rabbits, and we reminisced about that last time, three years ago, when it wasn't like this. We went over it again, how it was better then, and Stuart was here then, and how the vermin were everywhere, and we played a game of eyes and quick reflexes, of rabbits and rapid response. We talked so hard we forgot we were spotting for rabbits.

So it seemed he appeared out of nowhere, a hundred yards ahead—a big male kangaroo standing tall in silhouette, almost humanoid. It might have been the shadow of a man, ripped out of shape by the travail of tearing itself free.

It made more sense as a shadow, a mirage. It was easier to imagine that than to accept how something so wild and grand could nourish itself and thrive on these starving acres. It would never have occurred to me that such a shadow could be shot at until Dave spoke, and he spoke quick:

"He's mine. This one's mine."

We had all stopped in our tracks.

"That's one hell of a rabbit." Rick giggled. I could tell he didn't quite feel right about it. His voice came out womanish. I glanced at Caleb. I couldn't read him.

After the kill, we didn't want to turn back to the house straight away. We made our way down to the dead creek, walking its broken back, Caleb trailing behind still refusing to judge. A scatter of rocks at our feet, streaked with what might have been fossils. We shuffled about in the sun too long, not wanting to be in the sun but not wanting to return, trying to make talk so we could just seem, just appear, to forget. Dave used the keywords *beer* and *television*, but it was a while before we turned back, and still the sun didn't seem to have moved.

...

We get pissed and more pissed and we keep the fire going and we try to keep the talk up because we have to talk over it, talk ourselves out of it, that roo. It wasn't all of us pulling the trigger, but when Dave called the shot I heard myself say *go for it*, and Rick owns the land, owns the two firearms, and he let it happen. So the three of us talk too much, making it sound as if we all feel like talking, and Caleb's the only one brave enough or clean enough not to say anything at all.

Rick tells the one about his dad and the Egyptian gymnast, and I hear myself guffaw, and I want to tell them one about my dad but nothing comes, which is no surprise, because Dad never had stories, and I don't like telling my stories because I'm afraid of being called smart, though Stuart always understood. Dave cracks his schoolboy jokes in descending order from bad to worse, from bad-taste to filth. Caleb misses his turn as he always does—taciturn—then it's my turn again and still there's nothing to say, no ready joke or anecdote, and all I can do is curse the insects.

There was going to be barbecue, but we drink on empty stomachs. We were supposed to be having rabbit. There are foil-wrapped leftovers inside, yesterday's, but I guess we're not hungry. There's drink.

Looking at Dave as he sits in the firelight with his bloody conscience and his face lit up all wrong, I remember the faces on those cheap little plastic figurines that came with my supermarket train set when I was seven. They were tiny, crudely molded, and whatever sweatshop worker had applied the paint had done so in such a rush that the mouth was a mere pink splash, the eyes two erroneous splodges not quite lining up with the plastic. That's Dave's face: a botch.

...

Because when we walked up to that felled kangaroo, it wasn't there. Something else had lain down in its place. Only we didn't know it yet.

Caleb wouldn't come with us, hanging back, but the rest of us were keen, and as we drew near, Dave was already calling out, "Sorry, big fella!" to his kill.

The thing lay sideways. It was the coat of the thing that first struck me—the soft depth of its ply, and colors in the fur like the memory of bushfires. Besides the blood. The tail was splayed.

He wasn't yet dead. But we were prepared for that. I was brave enough to stand there while he looked back us. For a moment I even thought his eyes were fixed on mine, proud and soundless and affirmative. We were prepared for that. We were so fixed at first on his eyes and the red wound in his neck with its trickle of blood that it took us a moment to notice his pouch.

Her pouch.

"She ... " said Dave.

I couldn't speak, though we had nothing to be afraid of. It was just movement in a bulging sack of skin. Just a horror of unthinkable slow motion. Just the shape of something inside there, waking, stretching its limbs in that impossibly flaccid bag.

Rick's voice shook. "It can't be," he said. "It couldn't, he, she—a female can't grow to that size."

Only she didn't look quite so big, up this close.

No one else spoke, but we didn't look away. She would look away first. She bore the wound peacefully, that mother, her breath slowly stilling in her sides even as the thing writhing out of her belly roiled harder. Long shading lashes swept her dark eyes, and she kept them open even when she stopped seeing us.

When we rejoined Caleb, he wasn't looking at us, but he fell in step when we turned back to the house. We started back at a pace unnaturally quick, and I wondered how much Caleb had seen.

About halfway back, Dave fumbled and dropped his rifle on his foot; the butt thumped the toe of his shoe.

"Shitbuggershit!" he shouted. "Bugger the bloody—ahh!"

"You right, mate?"

"Bugger the buggery—Jesus! Yeah, I'm fine. Ahh. I'm fine."

. . .

Now it's the scotch bottle. The stuff tastes good, full of heat, though it must be a cool night by now. It's only with the fifth swig that I notice the pain in my mouth, flaring sharp, and I realize that, at some point, I have bitten my tongue.

Rick's on a roll, remembering his father's various cars and their various mishaps. He's too drunk to talk straight, but it's still good. Now and then his voice fades, hot air rises through it, but he rallies and keeps up the thread.

He has to, and we have to help him. Because it doesn't take much figuring to work out how three men brave enough to shoot a defenseless herbivore could be too cowardly to wring her joey's neck. And it doesn't take too much working out to figure how three men that cowardly could lack bravery enough to talk about it. They're out there still, of course: that big thing lying dead, and the little thing that might not quite be dead yet, that might still be waving, drowning in the cold milk of loss. But we are boxed up safe in the firelight drinking and laughing, safe even from silence. So whatever is out there is behind us, lost in the day, as irrelevant as two sneakered feet on a beach. Sand packed down hard in the hourglass.

Except that there's Caleb. I look across at him. His mouth is a thin, ruled line, and he's still got that poor bottle by the neck, and I wait for him to look up at me, but he doesn't, though I wait long. The other two are singing. My voice is in there somewhere, too, rising through the deaf-mute eucalypts. My tongue is stinging, still. In the dark, through the thin, bitten skin, I can taste the shadow of my blood.

Dry quarter hours. Dark half hours. As I fill it up with drink, my head runs empty. It's not just an absence of thought—it's the actual presence of emptiness. It's as if I can't think of anything to think. In the dark at once vast and close, I wander my inner catacombs in search of stories and find them filled in by the airless dark.

There's only one thing that rears up, grotesque in its exaggerated outlines, twisting about side-to-side in the fur like a Claymation, a broken animatronic.

There must be air because we're breathing. Must be something. Time, at least, to put between us. Because the day is long gone with the light and so the distance is gone, too—contracted to this campfire ring, with that bottle-top moon overhead. It's all we have left: We are blackboxed in time.

...

The descent of men is so enthralling I barely notice myself descending. For a while we are barely human. I never realized before how much it hurts to laugh, then I don't notice anymore because his face is in my face, full of big teeth and the tongue slicked with something, a broth of beer spit and phlegm, then I see Rick loping like the missing link, and Dave has let go of my collar and I see him adrift and I drink and then someone mentions Stuart and then I'm angry because it's too much like talking about the kangaroo.

Against the tide of dry heat, Dave's voice pushes louder and louder. "It wasn't me, you know, I mean, it wasn't my idea! And how was I supposed, and how were we supposed—it wasn't me! How were we supposed to know?"

So he's decided to name it now—it's started; it's all coming out. He keeps screaming it at Caleb, his words aimed point-blank at Caleb's face, which stays shut tight, though the bottle has dropped from his hand. Then Dave and Rick clash because Rick doesn't want to hear it any more than I do, and Dave's rant goes on beneath Rick's roar while Judge Caleb's mouth remains a rigid rule, but it no longer matters who says what or hits who because even Caleb must be drunk by now and I think I'm already drunk enough not to remember this night in the morning. I taste blood and it's not just my tongue this time, it's my lip. Rick has busted my lip, which makes no sense at all because isn't it Caleb we're s'posed to be stifling?

I have forgotten the postcode for Ithaca. I no longer know what's going on. All I know is that whatever is happening shouldn't, and I have to keep watching their faces to work out what I'm saying and doing from their reactions because I can't even think what I'm thinking.

If the morning ever comes, there may be peace, and then it will come up behind me—guilt, the white bunyip. It will lay its clay hand on my shoulder and summon me away to a place dim and unforgiving, that HATCHERY, and my wife will be there staring at me over her laptop with the long-lashed eyes of a kangaroo.

But for now there are too many stars, the sky a huge glitter-filled snowdome and this little plastic Aussie outback just glued in the bottom. It's filled with liquor and I don't know if it's him or me or them or who talking when I start hearing how it hurts too much *it hurts I'm not sure who or what's saying it* hurts it hurts it hurts *the bush voices littering the air and I can only try to guess, guess, and guess.*

And lying on my back seeing the sky for real with those million stars I notice that the moon is gone, which is good because it means time, time, time, and if there were a million coral insects up there, as many as stars, they could finish the job—twitch and tweak their microscopic pincers, macerate all this, breaking it down and us, too, then build it anew. I'm happy in my drink and on my back with my broken thinking, for my memory has fragmented into quiet archipelagos—just the odd atoll of hate or fear left jutting up now, as irrelevant as two sneakers. Because the sea is forgetting. You look out over it, the blue blank, and things sink. And that's the desert.

It Won't Be Long Now

JoeAnn Hart

BELINDA HEAVED HERSELF upright in bed at the sound of a prolonged wail. Then silence. In the dark, the blinking red light on the monitor told her the unit was on, but not whether her daughter was breathing. The next pained cry seemed to come from all directions at once, and she could not locate it even as she stumbled blindly toward Rowan's room. At the open door she held her breath and tried to listen over her own heartbeat, a red wave pounding against her brain.

"Nothing," she whispered, more in hope than anything else. No life-or-death fight for air this time.

She gathered herself together in the doorway, where for so many nights she'd slept on her feet like a horse. It had been a warm September and wet besides. The humid air that made the toilet paper damp and magazines curl also encouraged the spores that were her daughter's mortal foes. Single-celled creatures that didn't even know if they were animal or vegetable could take her down like gunshot. Belinda kept a trigger list on the refrigerator, but it might as well read *The World*. Not only mold and mildew spores but pollen from trees, grasses, and weeds; exercise; exposure to cold dry air or hot humid air; industrial emissions; vehicle exhaust; smog; and other air pollutants. *Strong emotions.* How could she protect her daughter from feelings? It would be easier to hold back the sea with a rope.

A dog bayed from across the mudflats, and Belinda snapped out of herself and crept to Rowan's side. Her breathing was raspy but steady, and Belinda's shoulders eased. Her own breath was still labored, but that was because of all the lard she carried around her *midsection*, as her doctor called it, as if she were a cut of beef. She hated the needy part of herself that made her reach for food when her own strong emotions had her by the throat.

The nightlight shone on Rowan, lighting up one side of her buttery, plump face. Ten years old and already *obese*, as they said in school. Now there was a word gone awry in the system. It used to be reserved for problem fatties; now it was attached to kids like Rowan who were merely on the pudgy side. Some of that—maybe a lot of that—was because Belinda was afraid exercise would trigger an asthma attack, so she kept her out of sports. No lean athletic body for Rowan. Not like her dad, the robust one. Yet he was the one who didn't make it. Jim was a fisherman in a fished-out sea. His captain had been forced to go farther and farther out, in all weather, to catch anything at all. On a day the birds were blown inside out like umbrellas, Jim got snagged by an untethered line and swept off the deck. The crew tried, but Jim never came up once. Not once. After a few unfathomable words from the Coast Guard, her future dissolved like salt in water. She buried an empty coffin and called him dead.

Belinda did not want to wake Rowan, but she could not

resist a single touch. She let her palm drop on her child's chest, just to feel it rise. Rowan's shoulder was moist beneath her Little Mermaid nightgown, and while Belinda pondered what that might mean, the banshee wail rose up again, and she pulled her hand away as if she'd been stung. But the unearthly sound hadn't come from her daughter, or even from inside the house. It—a deer? coyote?—was in the backyard. The noise was so alien it could even be a bear. They hadn't been seen in coastal Massachusetts in a hundred years, but then again, neither had coyotes, and yet they'd reinvented themselves as suburban pests. Nothing seemed impossible anymore when it came to nature. But whatever "it" was, it was in trouble. The barks and gasps were like the worst of Rowan's attacks, the ones that sent them to the ER for a few hours on the nebulizer.

Rowan rolled over with a grunt but did not wake up. Belinda tiptoed out of the room and back to her own. She looked at the clock. Four a.m. The hour of the wolf, as Jim used to say—the time he got up nearly every day of his life. She pulled a sweatshirt over her head and stood at the window, staring out into the gray world of the salt marsh, where no artificial light reflected off the water. The moon was long gone. The plaintive moans continued, so there was no use trying to get back to sleep. She held the nylon curtain like a security blanket against her face and waited for the sun to catch up with her. The outbursts continued, less frequently but more disturbing, like something out of a horror movie. "What *are* you?" she asked. A young animal calling for its mother? An old one pushing hard against the inevitable?

In time, the first yellow glow of the sun began to organize the yard into light and dark. She watched featureless birds shake themselves awake in the branches and fly off. The house cast a long shadow. By the fence, the sunlight fell on the broken swing set with its cracked slide and Rowan's turtle-shaped sandbox, things she'd long outgrown but they had not known how to get rid of. The same with the lobster boat up on a wooden cradle. It was shrouded in a tarp streaked with gull shit, and the keel was hairy with dried green slime. A boat out of water was a sorry thing. Belinda kept putting it on Craigslist, hoping for a nibble, but it was too far gone. Jim had bought it cheap to fix up and start lobstering, since apparently there were still bugs for the catching. Mostly, though, he'd wanted to stay closer to shore for Rowan's sake. So much for that.

She realized that the morning had become silent, and the silence was nothing short of ominous. The sun rose higher, making the house shadow shorter, letting her see farther down where the yard began to morph into tidal marsh. She squinted her eyes. "What the … ?" A black lumpen form. A giant trash bag? It was too far up on the lawn to have come floating in at high tide. Maybe someone got rid of a dog, or even a litter of puppies, tossed like garbage in her yard. It made her sick to her stomach. She was glad it was Saturday so she could take care of it one way or another before Rowan woke up. She didn't want her to know the worst about the world.

She pulled her shell pants over her pajama bottoms and slipped on Jim's old rubber boots. They were too big, but they worked, and she could not afford to replace anything that still worked. Her job at the diner paid for shit. The little bit of insurance money had run out, and she was wearing out her welcome at the Fisherman's Widows and Orphan Fund. She closed the back door quietly behind her and picked her way down the slope toward the marsh. There had been a mean downpour a few days before. The lawn still squished with the weight of her step. The air had that murky morning stink, and the shadows were so dense she was surprised she could even walk through them.

She stopped at the woodpile to grab a stick of kindling, just in case. There was plenty of it. Their poorly insulated house had been mostly heated by wood, with just a few electric baseboard heaters that she could not afford to turn on. But Rowan's doctor said no more wood stove. "How can she be allergic to wood smoke?" she'd asked him. "Didn't humans evolve with it? Didn't fire jump-start civilization?" He'd shrugged. "Maybe we're devolving," he'd said, with a chuckle. This was the same doctor who told her to get air-conditioning to keep Rowan from coughing up garden slugs, but he did not tell her how to pay for it.

Holding on to her stick, she approached the bag with caution. In the half-hearted light, she saw the bag move. She stopped about twenty feet away. She hadn't thought about how she could safely open the bag. She patted her pants. No phone. That was dumb. As she was wondering if she should just go back and call the police, the pointy end of the bag lifted up and stared at her with mournful eyes.

"A seal? Are you a harbor seal?" She looked around as if the answer were to be found in the reeds. He was far from home, separated from the sea by miles of marsh. She turned back to this baby-faced animal, still not quite believing it. "What are you doing here?" The seal lowered his head but kept his eyes on her as she inched closer. His dove-gray body was mostly neck and chest, and his head was like a peeled egg with whiskers. As she got closer still, she caught the scent of deep ocean on him, the way Jim used to smell at the end of a long trip.

She stood still, not knowing quite what to do, and as the sun rose, she saw that the seal had deep cuts all over his body, and his stomach was raw. "Poor thing," she said. He must have been pulling his blubber on land for some distance. If he was not exactly dying, he was as near to it as to make no matter. She took a step toward him, still clutching her stick, and he lunged toward her with a snap of his yellow teeth.

She jumped back. "Okay! I get it." Because of Rowan, she'd gotten so used to seeing seals as cute plush toys or cartoon figures; she'd forgotten what they were really like. At the town dock, they lounged on their backs, eating live lobsters they'd stolen from traps, holding the struggling crustaceans between two flippers like ice-cream cones, crunching through the shells with a bite that could tear off your face.

...

A man from the Aquarium, with rimless glasses and a dense beard, looked down toward the estuary. The sky was an even dead white, and the air was warm. It was autumn only by the falling leaves of the swamp maples. "He hauled himself all the way up here?"

Belinda shrugged. "He started making a fuss sometime after I went to bed. I thought it was a human crying or something."

"They can be like that." A woman from the rescue team put down her satchel. "When explorers first landed on Cape Cod, the sailors thought the seals were mermaids, calling to them."

"Want to hear a mermaid joke?" asked Rowan, shyly.

Belinda wished Rowan had stayed up at the house. The yard was lousy with wet leaves, and she could smell the spores blooming at their feet. The "aspergillosis monster," she and Rowan called the fungus. Besides which, this whole thing might end poorly. But how could she keep Rowan from seeing the seal? Rowan loved animals, yet they could not have a dog, and a cat was out of the question. And here, an animal appears right in her yard. A sick animal, but a real one.

"Shoot." The woman studied the seal with a squint, walking around his six-foot, tapered body. She was almost as tall as the seal was long, but she was thin as an eel. She wore jeans and a T-shirt and was so tan she had sunburnt eyelids. Belinda was glad she'd made the effort to change out of her dumpy sweats and put on a nice shirt and jeans, even though they were so tight she could barely breathe and her cell phone in her pocket dug into her hip. She even put on her good sneakers, knowing they'd get soaked in the grass. For some reason, she had wanted to make a good impression on these people. Same as Rowan, apparently.

"Okay," said Rowan, squeezing her hands together. "A man and a cat are on a desert island. They see a mermaid on a rock. The man imagines the mermaid as having a pair of legs, and the cat imagines her as all fish."

The tan woman laughed, causing Rowan to squeal with delight. Belinda worried laughing would lead to coughing.

"That's a good one," said the bearded man. "We only see what we need, don't we?"

A man in a hoodie and flip-flops was crouched down near the seal. "Maybe we should just put him out of his misery," he said. "He's in a pretty bad way."

Belinda made a face at him and shook her head.

"Misery?" said Rowan, softly.

"Why is it here?" asked Belinda, to switch the subject.

"Look." The woman pointed to his tail. "Fishing filament wrapped around his hindflippers and tail."

"You know what the monkey said when it backed his tail into the lawn mower?" asked Rowan. Everyone stared at her. "It won't be long now."

"That's not funny," said Belinda. The two men made polite ha-ha mutterings and went about their business, but the woman looked concerned, obviously wondering what child would joke in response to a distressed animal. Rowan had developed a sick sense of humor since Jim died. Her counselor at school told Belinda it was her way of distancing herself from pain.

"The seal couldn't use his flippers to swim," the woman explained, as if Rowan's problem was that she hadn't understood the situation. "Looks like he got pretty battered when the tide pulled him in through the marsh channels. It's a wonder he didn't drown."

"He can't drown," said Rowan. "He lives in the water."

"He's a mammal, like us," said the bearded man. "He can hold his breath longer, but he still has to come up for air. If he can't swim, he sinks."

"Probably why he was trying to escape above the tide line," said the flip-flop boy. "He's a fighter, I have to give him that."

"Well, let's give him a chance then," said the bearded man, dialing a number on his phone. The tips of his fingers were flat, like a frog's. "I'm going to try to snag a boat and move him that way. He'll be less stressed. Besides, we'll never get the rescue unit out of this muck if we bring it down here."

"Then someone would have to rescue the rescue unit, right?" said the tan woman, making Rowan giggle. "Let's get this line off him first. Jason, go get the halter."

"Will he get better?" asked Rowan.

"We'll see what we can do for him at the Aquarium," said the woman. "He might just need a few stitches and some rest."

Belinda didn't believe a word of it. None of them looked as if they really expected him to live. The seal was watching them, and Belinda thought there was a wordless intelligence behind those big eyes that knew it, too.

The bearded man put his phone away. "The harbormaster will meet us at the dock. He's got a sweet little inflatable with a lift for us, but he said we might have to wait a bit for the tide to turn to enter the marsh."

Jason came back with a canvas halter, letting it fall over the seal, tightening the straps to keep him still. The seal did not lunge at them the way he had gone at Belinda, and she was a little put out by that. The woman slipped on rubber gloves that went up to her elbows, protective goggles, and a surgical mask. The kind Rowan had to wear on high-pollen days.

"What are you afraid of catching?" Belinda asked, alarmed about a possible new danger for Rowan.

The woman took a pair of curved scissors out of her satchel. "It's not for me. It's to protect the seal from any germs *I* might have. He's got a lot of open sores." She began to snip away the tangle of line. "What a mess. I think there's a hook embedded, too." The seal twitched, and Jason was having some trouble controlling him with the straps. He stood on the end of one so he could use all his strength holding the others.

"This is all we've done for days," said the bearded man, grabbing one of the straps to help Jason. Belinda pulled Rowan back. "A storm out to sea worked up these lines that just float around catching sea mammals like our buddy here. Mostly we've just been counting the dead."

As she watched the Aquarium people work, Belinda was touched that they would go to all this trouble to try to save the seal. She ought to try as hard to save herself. She looked around at the broken toys and unused boat, the vinyl clapboards peeling off the back of the house. Belinda became painfully aware of how shabby her life must look to them. Since Jim died, she had not kept up with the repairs of the house. She had not taken care of so many things, and now it was all falling down around her.

Rowan coughed and then tried to stifle the next. She took her inhaler out of her pocket and took a hit, then another.

"Come on, you," Belinda said to Rowan. "Grandma's going to be here soon to pick you up."

Belinda's parents both smoked, so Rowan could never go to their house, but they went on road trips sometimes. Today they were going to the mall to buy some school things, and they knew not to smoke in the car with Rowan. They'd learned that lesson the hard way the last time they took her shopping, when they ended up at the ER instead of the Gap. Belinda was going to go along, but now she thought she'd stay and make sure things went smoothly with the seal. Maybe she could be of some help.

"Just stay away from the seal while we're gone," said the flip-flop boy. "He wants to rest, and a human presence could send him over the edge."

"Don't worry," said Belinda, once again feeling a little put out. It was her seal, after all. It was her yard. "Rowan's off for the day with her grandma, and I've got work to do around the house."

"What?" asked Rowan. "What work? I thought you were coming with us."

"Off we go!" said Belinda, patting her daughter on the bum to get her moving. They hiked back up the slope to the house, neither of them breathing pretty.

In the end, Belinda couldn't help herself. After Rowan and her parents drove off, and after having explained to her mom, yet again, how to use the emergency call feature on Rowan's phone, she sat at the kitchen table with a coffee mug and looked out the window. The tide was slack, and the seal was quiet. Maybe he was feeling better now that the line had been cut away from his tail. Or maybe he'd just given up.

"You must be hungry," she said out loud. She heaved herself out of the chair and made two tuna sandwiches, one for her and one for him, stacking them on a paper plate. She found Rowan's unbreakable cereal bowl and covered them with it, then grabbed a plastic water bottle out of the refrigerator and tucked it under her arm. "Okay, then," she said, and carried the picnic down to her salty visitor.

She was still wearing her sneakers, so she slipped a bit on the wet lawn going down to the marsh. The seal seemed to study her progress, as if wondering how a land animal could be so clumsy on land. She squatted close to him, but not too close. She remembered his pointy teeth. As she bent, she felt the waistband of her jeans slice into her flesh, so she unsnapped her top button and released her breath. "That's better," she said. She threw one of the tuna sandwiches to the seal, half expecting him to catch it mid-air like at Sea World, but it landed in pieces by his clawed flippers. She poured some water into the bowl and pushed it toward him with the piece of kindling, getting it as close as she dared. The seal gave her a look of warning, and she backed off, settling herself on the ground well out of reach. She wished she'd brought a folding chair with her. The ground was damp, and she was not sure she could stand back up without help. She had to take her phone out of her pocket and put it next to her in order to get comfortable at all.

She dug into her sandwich, but the seal did not even look at his. "I know," she said, chewing. "I wish I had chips, too. Maybe a pickle." But it wasn't funny. He seemed worse off than before, even without the fishing line. He wasn't moving and didn't blink. Maybe the flip-flop boy was right and he was too far gone after all.

Belinda finished her lunch in a few bites and sighed. It was sad about the seal, but it was nice to be outside doing nothing. She rarely got to just sit. The warmth of the day made her sleepy. Even the wind was drowsy. Nearby was a circle of smooth beach stones with a charred center, all that was left of a few fine summer evenings, where, if Rowan stayed upwind of the smoke, they would sit outside and consider the stars. But the last time they'd had a campfire, Rowan had woken up in the middle of the night in trouble, so they hadn't done it since. It was getting so Rowan could no longer take part in the natural world. Maybe they should do what the doctor suggested and move to Arizona, where the desert air was too dry for spores, and the schools were air-conditioned. But Belinda couldn't imagine leaving this place. It was all she knew.

She looked at the seal. The tuna sandwich sat untouched, attracting flies, some of which began to settle on his wounds.

She slowly stretched toward him to wave them away with her paper plate, and he bared his teeth at her. His breath smelled like a ship's hold, and she stopped. She wanted to say she was sorry—about the fishing line, about the flies, about everything—but he did not want her sympathy.

"Suit yourself," she said. It's what she got for trying to help. She should just leave him alone and go back to the house, but some instinct would not let her leave his side. He was stranded, just like her. She was a bit seal-shaped herself, with almost the same number of chins. They were both full-blooded mammals, distant cousins, for better or worse. Here was a species who used to live on land but had decided against it. For some reason, the seals had chosen to go back to the sea. She wondered if they regretted that decision, now that the water was getting as dangerous for the seals as the land was for Rowan. In the meantime, the die was cast for them all. If he survived, he would return to his element. She imagined him healed and healthy, striking out for the sea, pushing himself along the sand with his muscular flippers, then merging with the water as if he and it were one.

Belinda wondered if going back would ever be an option for humans. It had not been an option for Jim. She flashed on his death, as she so often did, his leg caught in the tangle of lines, the frightening change from air to water, him twirling in the green gloom, the panic as he tried to reach for the knife in his belt, then the horrific awareness that it was too late. The vastness of the ocean was nothing compared to the finality of death. She hoped he experienced a moment of beauty before it all went dark, that he felt embraced by the water, swimming in love, as if he were coming home at last.

"Life is a struggle against death, my friend," she said to the seal. The light was dimming. The rescue team had better hurry, with the days getting shorter. She looked at the marsh, and the water seemed high enough for the boat to enter the channel. "Soon," she said to the seal. "Very soon." Her mind became silent as she stared at him, admiring the perfect arched line of his body, the puppy-dog eyes. He was truly a beautiful being of the sea. When he turned his head away from her, she did what they told her not to do. She shuffled closer to him on her butt, then reached over and touched him.

Who knew such a large animal could move so fast? She felt the bite in slow motion, the slice through her muscles, teeth against bone, veins and arteries opening wide to the world, coloring it red. The pain was so vivid it did not even register. When she got free, she hugged her arm to her body and would not look at it. The seal was more alert than he'd been all day, arching back like a snake. She felt warmth soak through her shirt and spread across her stomach, and she lay down on her side.

Fear deadened her voice. She could not cry out for help, but she could hear everything with a clarity she hadn't even known existed. Off in the distant harbor, the sound of the sea was like a breathing thing. She heard the peals of church bells in town, the brass sound reverberating softer and softer until it was just a whisper. Then she realized that it was not a church bell but her phone, lying in the weedy grass, vibrating and flashing red. She envisioned her mother in the ER with Rowan but could not pick it up. She would meet them soon enough. She heard the mechanical hum of the boat as it hydroplaned over the marsh, and the great marsh birds flapping away at its coming. She could almost smell its exhaust. She imagined the blades of the boat's propeller cutting through the water toward her, and the spray rising up to the sky in front of the prow, the vessel leaving a splendid hollow in its wake. "We're saved," she whispered to the seal, even though she didn't believe a word of it. "Saved."

She closed her eyes, and in the darkness the animal made a noise that froze her to her core.

Bight, Tomcat, and the Moon

Carmen Marcus

I'M ME, BIGHT. I'm wearing my dad's old smock flecked with fish scales and white with salt lines. I'm barefoot on road dust. I'm thirteen and a girl, double bad luck if you're a fisherman, but I'm not. I'm the keeper of the Last Sea on the road, and it's time to rock the boat.

Moon's as full as she'll get since the Big Ebb—just a fish-scale sliver—since humans went walking all over her face in their fat white boots, then probes to study her plumes. Enough's enough, so she cut her ties and drifted, taking the sea with her. My father, a fisherman, caught the last of the sea, scooped her up, fish and all, into the Seahouse. "Stick to the roads," he said, "and steer clear of ghost currents." So now I'm the moon to my finny friends, the tidal pull of my tiny sea until I find the true blue.

The Seahouse is two boats stuck together, one on top of the other like pursed wooden lips. The bottom house is where the last of the fishes live. The top house is where I live. I sleep over water, so I always dream of floods. The Seahouse balances on an A-frame pulled by the tractor. Tonight, I'm hanging from the starboard side shucking the Seahouse so it bounces on its big rubber tires. Fish love moon-rock nights. The whelks tuck their spiny legs inside their shells and let themselves roll. The big monkfish totters on his tiny pectorals across the beam. The mackerels—well, they're the first to go moon-mad, flashing their forked tails at the sky. I can hear the water slapping up the insides of the boat like a crowd going wild. As I swing up over the gunwale I see the anemones spurt their firework colours. Ha ha. Little punks.

I don't show the Sink folks this bit; moon-rock nights are just for us. But they are for show—my scaly, spiny underwater friends. Maybe I shuck too much tonight. I got a belly-full-of-broken-glass ache, and three red blood spots drop onto the road dust between my feet. I can't get sick like my dad; I got promises to keep. So I stick to the old black roads like he said.

There it is—the smoking stack of a Sink. A wheezing twist of humans squatting round underground pools. Sinks don't have names or signposts. Proper names are for things that will last or be remembered. I roll up.

"Remember the days when there were still fish in the oceans and cars on the road?"

I give it a good lung holler over the tractor engine and clang the mast bell.

"Come see, come see—the one, the only, the wet, the weird, the Last Sea on the road."

They used to pay when it still stung that the moon pulled away and the whole ocean buggered off down a crack in the earth. But tonight, when I let them climb up the big treads of the wheels, they peer through the portholes, and what they mostly feel is disappointed. They rub their coins in the red dust of their pockets and keep the water pots they promised for a look. Fish is fish, scales and gills. What more do they want? Mussels click. Urchins sting. "So ugly," they said. "Don't even make us hungry." Well, screw you. My friends aren't for eating.

The Sinkers like the saltwater battery best. It's just an old plastic box I use to test the water salinity like my dad showed me. Seawater is alive because of the salt. All the colored bulbs light up like a birthday cake. "Aww," they go. But tonight only seven lights light. My water's dying, and I don't know what I'm going to tell the fish. They flutter their gills at me just the same. I dunk my head under and I tell them so the Sinkers can't hear.

"I'm just a thirteen-year-old kid. I don't know shit about how to read the stars or get you home."

Mickey Fin poofs his cool blue lips on my fingertip. Kiss. Kiss. There's a ripping inside of me, way past guilt. If this is it—current-struck—I've had it. Can't be, 'cause I never even seen so much as a dust twitch of a real ghost current. I pick Mickey up and get the battery, and I push my way into the shouts and reaching hands wanting to touch the silver fish. They think this is some new show.

Inside the Sink reeks. Water's too precious for washing bodies in here. I swim every day. I must smell like every summer holiday they ever had. Makes them go funny. 'Specially the men, but I'm thirteen, pale and titless as the moon. I've tested Sink water before, but there's very little life in it even though it's been through so many people. There's a wall of big blokes round the pool, ghouls mirrored in its wet eye—Clonks we call 'em—their blades are made from old garden spades, and you don't want a clonk from one of them.

"Wait your turn."

There's a mucky sort of order in the Sinks.

"Don't want to drink, I want to test. I've got fish. They could live in your Sink."

"Don't want fish piss in my pool."

Here's the Sink King now. So I show him Mickey Fin, who's got his wriggle on now he's sussed the air's too light to push through his gills. Sorry, Mickey. The Sink King nods, curious, and I dip my battery in. All the lights light up, and of course I get an "Aww" from the crowd. Their dust-raw eyes prick up at the pretty lights. Idiots. Then it's little Mickey's turn. I seen him grow from an egg into the squiggles on his back, like I wrote my name on him. I seen him tickle his way out of Dora Crab's black claw. He's a survivor. He's straight in—I don't see him, just the ripple he leaves behind. No one's breathed for a whole minute now. Then his silver half-moon belly tips up in the black water. I wade in, slipping past the Clonks. He's not moving. Sorry, sorry, sorry, Mickey. The Sink King's laughing and stoking his brazier for a fish supper. He tries to take Mickey right out of my hand. No way am I letting go. I kick the fire, and the dust in the air sparks. The Clonks are busy trying to put out their King, and I'm off.

I'm almost at the Seahouse when these red fast hands snatch Mickey right out of mine.

"Give me back my fish."

Mickey's so small, curled nose to tail on the pink pad of a paw. This bloke is a real ginger scruff, a cheeky Tomcat. I heard of Purrmen but never seen one close. I heard after the Big Ebb folks would eat anything—their own pets and worse. But the problem with cats is they got nine lives, and at least seven came bursting back through the skins of those what ate them. Purrmen—whiskers and claws and triangles for ears.

"Where you heading in that?" he says, whistling at the Seahouse through a smile full of pins.

"The sea," I say.

"You won't get there by road. You know your stars?"

This is a bone of contention as my dad was supposed to show me how to sail by the stars. He said he'd teach me when

I was older. I got older. He didn't. He got taken by a ghost current, struck so bad he looped a knot around his own neck just to keep his water still.

There's a loud, angry noise coming from the Sink. I rev up the tractor.

"Take me with you," he meowls, a cool rumble that hushes my bellyache. "And I'll teach you your stars."

He climbs up, Mickey still coiled on his palm, and I don't stop him, but I make sure this cat knows:

"Mickey's not for eating."

. . .

Inside the bottom house, the Purrman looks less ginger. He's got poor little Mickey by the tail, dunking him in the water, but Mickey's silver's coming back. Mickey pulls himself free and sulks, hiding in the dead-man's-fingers.

"What's your name?"

"Tomcat." I have to laugh. "What's yours?"

"Bight."

"What? *Bite* like *bit*?" He snaps his teeth closed, a perfect fit. "What kind of name is that for a girl?"

"It's my name. It's the bend in a rope before you make the knot. It's the beginning."

That's what my dad told me. It's still a rubbish name for a girl. My mum didn't get a say as she died having me. Dad kept her magazines so's I'd learn how to be a proper lady, but how's a girl called Bight supposed to cascade?

Tomcat looks in my sea just to see himself, checking out his ginger whiskers. Dora Crab's a soft-shelled tart; she blows him love bubbles, but he don't even blink.

"What d'you know about the sea?"

"You don't do much small talk, do you?"

I keep quiet long enough to prove his point. He takes off his shirt. I get my knife.

"Steady," he says, 'cause he wants me to see his scars. "You heard of ghost currents? That's where I got these."

"Heard enough to steer clear."

"Well, we won't find the Lost Sea on the road. Look up."

He tilts my head to the sky.

"That's the North Star. The stillest point in the sky. Stick out your arms."

He gets behind me, resting his chin on my neck, and I can feel the rolling instrument of his purr under his fur.

"Your right hand is east, your left west. Keep watching the star."

He spins me round so his words fill the tickle cup under my chin.

"We're going south."

I daren't look down; the star is the only part of me that's still.

. . .

My bellyache's gone. Moon's as round and black as Tomcat's eyes. He's cleaning his whiskers like he's ready to eat, grinning at the old magazine pictures of women on my walls.

"What you got these for? You like girls?"

I punch his arm. I can't explain these women—their quiet lips, the heavy swells of their women's bits under silk. I look for them in my hurting body, certain they will never come. I seen this world curling up in knots to die and me—I'll be stuck at bad-luck thirteen forever. I draw my mother's empty makeup brush across my cheek, and my eyes light up like the saltwater battery. I always wanted a ginger Tom to curl up on my lap so I could rub the red velvet of his ears.

. . .

I find Dora Crab's lonely black claw in Tomcat's bed. I throw it at him, and he catches it and slowly blinks his eyes, leaning into a kiss.

"It's my nature," he says.

"It's my boat," I say and lose my fingers in his fur to push him overboard.

Then we hit something—the big old bones of a wreck. I pull on my mother's old silk skirt up over the bare angles of my hips, and it shines like I'm walking in water. For the first time I feel the soft pinch and sink of sand under my feet, between my toes. A stray wind rasps it against my bare legs like a cat's tongue. I take a handful in my pocket for the fish. There's no sign of Tomcat.

The wreck is nothing like the Seahouse; dried up mermaid's purses still cling to her, clams guard her crumbling belly. I see she's got a name, *Queenie*, like a girl-cat. The sand bed swirls and lifts me off my feet—ghost current. Up I go, and then it throws me against the wreck. Tomcat's there; he catches me, tearing my mother's skirt. His fingers curl around my ribs.

"I've got you, kid." But the current's got us both, spinning us in the muscle of its memory. I take Tomcat's shoulder, and we could be dancing in the roll of the ghost sea. Death. That's what I'm thinking as I tipple topple into Tomcat's blue eyes. There's the sea, and he's had it all this time, locked up frozen in the ice flecks of his eyes.

"Let me go," I tell him as he topples me, and I hook my heel around his foot, forgetting how easy it is to hold on to something that doesn't have scales. But the current rips me— "Aiyee"—and lickety-splits me to pieces.

"You got properly current-struck, kid."

I'm shucked up all right—my head is empty, dark and

tumbling, not a twitch of a still star in my head. I can feel the ghost of his long claw on my ribs, bruising. It's a good deep-down grown-up kind of hurt that I need cool water to fix. I drop into the bottom house and they scatter, like they can taste it on me. The memory of their water. They nip at the bruises blooming on my ribs with questions I can't answer, and I wonder how Tomcat really got his scars.

"Throw him overboard," they say, Dora tapping her one good claw. I can't tell them that we need him because I've lost my still-north.

I dream of floods and wake up with sand in the creases of my sheets.

. . .

We roll further south, and still no sign of sea, just the abyssal plain stretched out like a warm cat. The moon spins, turning her face round, fuller than I've ever seen her. My bellyache's back and wakes me up. Rock-the-boat time no matter what. I hold on to the gunwale and shuck until my knuckles are white. Only Mickey Fin's riding the sweep 'cause no one else feels like bouncing. I slip into the bottom house while the waves are still pulsing.

"Come on," I say, but the mussels don't click, and I can taste their quiet death. Monkfish sulks at the bottom, and Dora looks like she's ready to be eaten. They float so still, so unlike the red current running through me.

"Dad," I said, like he wasn't dust, and I picture his big hands looping the first knot in the rope. "You shouldn't never have called me Bight"—and now I know it I cut my own red rope and jump in, mixing my water up with the Last Sea, saltwater filling up my nose.

Tomcat's face floats above me, a second moon. He has me

by my silk skirt. His white teeth flash, and he pushes his own breath into me, whiskery prickles around my lips. He tips me over his knee and slaps my back. I'm so mad he's made me begin again I push him in the deep end, and he yowls. He can't swim. His eyes—blue, black—flicker as his lungs panic and gulp wingfuls of water. So I haul him up and punch his ribs for Dora as he coughs.

"Trust me," he says.

"Ha," I say, then shut up 'cause I hear this *shush shush*. I've never heard it before; it's like the earth breathing.

On the horizon, the red head of the sun crests, setting fire to an impossible blue line. I put on my mother's silk dress for this, ready to meet the sea, the red sun pressing on our backs. But the sea is trapped; a steep canyon lies between us. There are a thousand lights moving up toward us from the drop. A tusky Purrman is the first to arrive, gray as dust. He slaps his paw around Tomcat and murowhs his hellos. The big old Gray-stripe thumps his paw on my boat. Dora Crab keeps quiet. Gray-stripe wears a coat of mackerel skin and a crown of mussel shells. He shines like the sea on the horizon. My finned friends know the moon is full, but they are still as they have ever been. They must taste their dead even through the wood.

"Good work, Tomcat. I'll give you five hundred for the boat."

"Five? You haven't seen the fish yet. That's the Last Sea you're looking at there—there's whelk and—"

"And three hundred for the girl."

My lips *pop pop* at the air like I'm still drowning, drawing at the nothing where water should be.

Tomcat nods and smiles, triangles for ears and a kiss full of pins. It is his nature. But I'm Bight, I'm the bend, I'm the beginning, I'm double bad luck. I am the bloody moon. I shuck, running from one side of the bottom house to the other. Those with legs run with me. The water lapping up and over the sides shouting *shush* to the other water sitting quiet at the horizon. I can feel the pull right under my ribs where my dreams of floods come from. The fist of the returning sea smashes the bottom house open. Wraps its wet paw around Tomcat, who is blowing kisses, his last, to me. I see my ocean come and pull him by his ginger tail.

...

The fish keep me alive and well in the upside down top house wrapped in a pocket of air. They promise me one day they will find land. I dream of cats' claws and my father's hands. These live currents wash away the memory of dust. Mickey asks me if I remember—

"The days long ago when there were still fish on the roads and dust for sea, there lived a young woman who would rock the boat."

He calls his friends to come and see the show. Clown fish bring him pearls to swim in my white hair. But he cannot make the water still on dark moon nights for me.

Phoenix Cross

C.S. Malerich

THE ONLY LOOK I EVER GOT at the full-blood phoenix was this photo Tommy sent from the lab. He said she's twice the length of a Heartfields Cobb—mostly the tail; the tail is real long, like a pheasant's—but half the body weight. Phoenix were never bred for meat, of course. They were never bred, period.

In person, she must be like a miracle come to life. Even in the photo, the feathers on top of the head are flaming orange, with red around the neck that gets darker and darker until the tail is black as coffee.

That wasn't the first time I envied Tommy. He always got to do things I didn't. College. Grad school. He even went skiing one Christmas.

...

I remember when Dad and Mom plowed over Gramps's spent cornfield to build the first grow-out barn. The whole county was going into chicken then because Heartfields had bought up the hatchery and the plant and modernized everything. They could process 2,000 birds an hour, which meant they wanted a lot of birds.

Not just any birds, though. Patented Heartfields Cobbs, engineered so their legs were perfect drumsticks and their breasts were perfect TV dinners. Plus, with the company's mix of supplements, they hardly ever got sick—Dad explained it all at dinner after the man from the company came around. Heartfields would supply everything, Dad said: the stock and the feed and the supplements. Eight weeks later, the company's trucks and the company's men would come get them. All we had to do in the meantime was make sure the automatic feeders were working. Gramps couldn't understand why such little birds needed a building as big as a football field, 'til Dad explained there'd be 20,000 birds in there.

"This is modern farming," Dad said. "Mechanized. State-of-the-art."

We'd get paid by the ounce, and then everyone, even us kids, could see why he'd signed on.

I was what, six? The spring before, Mom was teaching me and Tommy to hit whiffle balls in that cornfield, but now I can't remember what it looked like before the barn went up. I can't remember a time when we couldn't see the shining Heartfields plant from our porch, or when the company trucks weren't most of the traffic on our road. And every eight weeks, give or take, they stopped at Gramps's cornfield—what used to be Gramps's cornfield—to pick up the birds we baby-sat for them.

It didn't turn out the way Dad thought.

The stock wasn't as healthy as the Heartfields man let on, and someone had to walk through the barn at least once a day, checking on the birds and clearing out the dead ones. In every flock, some died of sickness or wounds, or just because they couldn't get to the feeding troughs and starved. Dad kept a tally next to the door of how many died that day. Sometimes flu hit, and we lost thousands.

Every dead bird counted against us once the company took and weighed them. After the trucks drove away, Dad and Mom would hose the shit and leftover carcasses into the lagoon at the end of the property. Then the barn would be empty for a couple days while we all held our breath.

Finally the Heartfields man would show up. He'd hand Dad the check that was always less than we hoped and a clicky pen to sign the contract for the next flock, already cheeping inside the trucks behind him. Dad hated to sign—I know he did, 'specially right after seeing that last check. But if he didn't, how were we gonna keep the lights on another two months?

"The next one will be better," he always said.

. . .

After Mom died, there wasn't any discussion about which of us would go to college. Tommy's grades were a hundred times better, and we didn't have the money to send us both.

"Maybe in a few years," Dad told me.

Well, in a few years, Tommy was in graduate school and Dad's lungs were sounding as bad as Mom's. So it was me who cleaned out the barn after the company trucks left. Me who picked up the leftover carcasses and hosed the chicken shit into the drains. Me who met the Heartfields man the next day with his check and his contract and his clicky pen. It was me who paid the bank and old hospital bills and Tommy's student loans. It was me watching us slip further and further into debt, all after building a state-of-the-art farm on Heartfields promises.

When we got the third bad flock in a row, I called Tommy.

Before I could say anything, he was telling me about the phoenix—a real live phoenix. Now him and his Abnormal

Biology team could study what made it resurrect. Something in the genes? Something in the environment? If they could break it down, step by step, that could change the future.

It all seemed very far away from the farm. I imagined him in a pristine lab, long white coat with shiny stainless-steel tools, learning how to make life re-make itself. It was like thinking about a different universe.

...

November was the first bad flock that year. I couldn't bring myself to tell Dad how bad.

Some of the stock died right off the bat; the rest clumped together under the heat lamps, making fluffy pyramids out of themselves. The ones that were too slow or too weak—well, they ended up on the bottom and got crushed. I got in there to try to clear out the dead ones and space out the live ones. They were dying so fast I'd find the bodies already putrefying. I puked a few times—more than a few times—and I have a pretty strong stomach.

Heartfields sent a field vet out to take a look. "They're cold," he told me. "Raise the heat."

...

"Every flock since Thanksgiving has been like that," I told Tommy. They came to us sick, and I could barely keep half of them alive to fatten up. I called Heartfields over and over. Field vets came out, and I followed their instructions every time: I turned up the heat because they said the stock was cold. Then I increased the ventilation because they said the stock was hot. Then I installed a new water system because they said the stock was dehydrated. We took on more and more debt and kept sending back fewer and fewer broilers.

And we weren't the only ones. Around here, people come off friendly until you ask something too personal, and then it's like a brick wall. But word was getting around town about problems with the Heartfields Cobbs. Mrs. Zwacky down the road had already gone bankrupt. I went to the estate sale and watched her sell everything in her house—the beds and the coffee table and the kitchen appliances, even that lawn ornament that looks like a woman bending over. Me and Tommy stole it for a prank once in high school.

No one said why she went bankrupt. No one had to. Bad flocks.

"I think the company's doing it on purpose," I told Tommy.

"How come?"

"It's the hens. Hens get older, their chicks get weaker. But they won't replace them now because the price of chicken is down. So they're stringing us along 'til the economy's better." If half the stock died, they didn't care; that was less chicken on the market to drive the price down and less they owed the growers. And they knew they could do it to us, too, because we're a Heartfields county. Hell, a Heartfields *region*. No other game in town.

I wanted to punch someone.

"They still have to feed the stock," Tommy said.

"Fuck that. The only thing cheaper than chicken is chicken feed."

Tommy whistled. "Quite a theory there, Joe. But you can't criticize the company. They'll cut you off."

There was no point in running up the phone bill to hear things I already knew. "One more bad flock," I told him, "and I'm gonna to have to choose—Dad's medicine or your student loans." Then I hung up.

He was the one to call back. You might've expected him to be angry or worried, but no.

"I have a solution for our problem." His voice was smiling, that usual stone-cold-cool smile of his, but I could tell he was serious for once. Really dead serious. That's when I started to hope.

"What?"

"It's what I've been working on out here," he said, getting close to the phone and speaking low. "Adding phoenix genes to the Heartfields Cobb."

. . .

A week later I got the photo of the phoenix. Two weeks later Tommy himself showed up in a refrigerated semi.

"Where'd you get the truck?" I asked.

"Grant money," he said, with that smile.

In the trailer were racks and racks of eggs. I was too wired to hold still, and I couldn't help picking one up. It was light, like someone had sucked the yolk out, but looks-wise, it was your average chicken's—brown as toast, with a few freckles. Just for a moment, I thought I felt movement inside, maybe responding to the warmth of my hand.

"Are you sure no one will be able to tell the difference?" I asked.

"They'll look just like Heartfields Cobbs on the outside," Tommy said. "Honest to goodness."

"And you're sure they won't, you know, explode?" All the stories I heard, this phoenix thing was playing with fire. Like real fire.

"Nah, Joe, it's been tested, over and over. The Crosses don't immolate themselves. You can slaughter them like any other bird."

Then he pulled out gloves and a mask from the truck's cab and asked me where to start.

We'd agreed to keep it between us two for now, like somehow that'd lower the risk. It didn't make me feel better, though, that we'd have to flush the Heartfields stock before we put the Cross eggs in the barn. Sick as they were, that stock was all that was standing between us and bankruptcy if Tommy's plan didn't work.

"You'd think I'd risk you and Dad and the farm if I wasn't sure?" he asked.

And me, I believed him. So we got started.

The grates over the drains came off easy, and then with rakes and shovels, we made piles of stock and pushed them in. They were cheeping as soon as we started, getting louder and louder as we went. It was almost deafening.

The thing is, when a chick cheeps, it never sounds like pain to me. It's some cutesy, cartoon noise. It definitely doesn't sound like a death scream, though I knew they were drowning and dying in there.

I stopped for a second to push sweat out of my eyes. Tommy had the hose, ready to flush them down the drains to the lagoons.

"Hey," he called to me. "They'd all be dead in eight weeks anyway."

I nodded. Then he turned on the water.

We didn't finish until dawn. Once the barn was clear, we put down the Cross eggs, turned up the heat lamps, and locked the doors. Tommy parked the semi behind the barn, where no one would see it from the road, and headed back to the university.

One egg I took home with me. I planned to put it back later, but for a little while I just wanted to look at it. Touch it. Maybe even see the chick when it came out.

I didn't sleep well that night. I kept dreaming I was trapped inside a small space, smaller than a closet, suffocating and trying to push my way out.

When finally I woke up Monday morning, the egg had hatched.

...

Chicks are always cute, I guess. I hadn't paid too much attention to them since I was a kid and they'd become a chore and then a product. This one, though—since it wasn't surrounded by thousands of others—this one I took some notice of. It was covered in yellow fluff, just the same as the chicks I was used to. It was restless, stretching its little legs and flapping its useless wings, slipping around the bottom of the plastic hamper where I'd put it. I laughed out loud a few times, just watching it.

Its beak made me nervous, though, when I looked hard. The chick had the usual scowling baby-bird face, but that beak was twice as long as normal. Was there something wrong with Tommy's gene-splicing? Then it hit me: I'd never seen chicks with their full beaks before. Heartfields always cuts them down to keep them from pecking each other and scarring the meat. I started to relax. We'd have to rig up something to de-beak the Crosses ourselves, but how hard could it be? The knuckle-draggers at the hatchery did it all the time.

As I was getting dressed, a sound rang out. I spun around. *Cheep!* It was the clearest note I'd ever heard, like a bell. *Cheep! Cheep!* It went on singing, and the craziest part was, I could have sworn some of the notes didn't come from the bird in my hamper.

Right away, I drove out to the barn. I didn't even have to unlock it. As soon as I got within earshot, I could have told you all of our eggs had hatched—the singing was that loud. We had a flock of Phoenix Crosses.

Shit, I thought.

. . .

"They sound like a fucking angel choir," I told Tommy on the phone.

"That's your imagination."

"They don't sound like normal chickens."

"Look, who's going to hear them? And if anyone does ask, just tell them I'm experimenting with the breed. Tell them Heartfields approved it." In the meantime, he said he'd talk to a friend in Ag Science about equipment for de-beaking.

No one asked. Dad never went down to the barn anymore on account of his lungs, and I think he was just happy to hear our new flock was healthy. It was the first day ever, in the history of the Jablonsky farm, that there wasn't one dead bird on the premises. Unless you count the flock of Heartfields Cobbs we'd flushed to the lagoons.

Which I guess you would.

I decided to keep the hamper chick, at least for a while.

"This because we never got you a dog?" Dad wheezed, his idea of a joke, when he found me feeding her. The only way to keep her quiet was to keep her fed.

"Just trying to learn more about them," I told him, the best I could come up with.

"Put it outside," Dad said. "They aren't housebroken."

But I kept the chick in my room for a week, even though the third day she flapped her way out of the hamper and ruined the rug with her shit and scratching. Hell, I never liked that rug anyway. I put a screen over the top of the hamper to keep her in after that, and I checked on her five times a day to make sure she hadn't figured a way out. The third night, she ate up all the Heartfields grain I'd brought from the farm, so instead of driving back out for more, I gave her table scraps. Bread crusts, apple cores, corncobs. That kind of thing. She pecked it up like it was a banquet.

. . .

Tommy brought the equipment for de-beaking, along with a couple of assistants. When it came to it, I didn't much like the idea of doing it ourselves, but he showed me the technique for holding a chick's head with your thumb so the nippers reach the beak. They were red-hot, cutting and cauterizing in the same stroke. At first I expected a bigger reaction from the chicks—and yes, they sang like a bunch of jingle bells right up to the moment they got their beaks sheared—but then they were quiet. I didn't know if they couldn't sing anymore, or if they just didn't feel like it.

There were so many for us to do, I got into the rhythm of the work and forgot to notice anything else.

When I got back to the house late that night, there was my chick, hopping around the hamper, singing for food. I'd forgotten about her, and she still had her beak, but I was done for the day. She could keep it. If I kept her apart from the others, she wouldn't get in any fights, and it wouldn't matter.

That night, I dreamt I had half my face burned off and woke up screaming. Dad came running and wheezing to find out what was wrong. From the hamper, the chick was still singing to me.

. . .

"Do these things have powers?" I asked Tommy on the phone.

He laughed. "They have a wholly unique biology that lets them resurrect themselves. Is that a 'power'?"

"Could they give me dreams?"

"You're having bad dreams?" He sounded surprised.

"Nightmares," I said. I was sweating. "I think it's the birds."

"Yeah, could be," he said, without giving it too much thought. "You're thinking about them a lot."

"No, Tommy, I mean the birds are *giving* them to me. Like on purpose. Like—the evil eye or something."

He laughed again. "Joe, they're just birds. Try sleeping pills."

. . .

By the end of the first week, my hamper bird sprouted white feathers like an ordinary Heartfields Cobb. I nearly took her down to the farm then, but instead I set up a coop outside the house with a screened-off run. There I could keep an eye on her, and maybe get a better night's sleep.

She got round and plump, with just that bright red comb to tell you that you were looking at a chicken and not a snowball. She was also strong, scratching and digging with her blue scaly feet, until all our grass was gone around the coop. Dad and me saw her dust-bathe from the porch. She'd scratch herself a basin in the ground and then flap and roll and get filthy dirty.

"You know, your great-granddad used to keep chickens," Dad told me.

"Yeah? Why didn't Gramps keep it going?"

"Not to sell. He had 'em for the eggs, and they ate up the pests in the garden. I used to name them."

"Name 'em? Like what were their names?"

"Oh, let me see … there was Pepper, uh … Spots. Um … oh, Sparky. Sparky was my favorite."

I laughed.

"What's this one?" Dad asked me.

I shrugged. "I don't know. She won't tell me."

Dad snorted his laugh and went back to watching.

If she wasn't digging, then she was flapping—launching herself from one corner to the other. Finally I did an experiment and let her out. She walked around the driveway, pecking and scratching and whistling—she never just clucked like a normal bird. She got into the garden and hopped in and out of Dad's wheelbarrow, and I kept an eye on her the whole time, wondering what the hell I'd do if I couldn't get her back into the coop. But at dinner she came back on her own.

I tried it a day at a time, and finally I just let her wander while the sun was up. I'd've worried about coyotes and raccoons, but I had a feeling she was a scrapper. She looked like a Heartfields Cobb, but she grew spurs on her feet, which I'd never seen on a hen, and she still had her beak, too. If there'd still been cockfights out at the Nablach barns, I think I might have taken her, just to see what kind of damage she'd do.

We were feeding the Crosses more than Heartfields rationed for their flock, so I knew we'd run out of feed before the eight-week cycle was up. Once the birds went hungry a couple days they'd lay their eggs. Tommy said that phoenix brood and prepare for their rebirth when food gets scarce or the climate gets harsh. The Phoenix Crosses would work the same way, he said.

Meantime, I saw my bird fatten up like the others. Every day, she moved less and less. I think she got too heavy for her own legs.

...

In my dream, I was restless. I wished I could scratch and dig, like my bird in the yard, and feel dirt under my nails. But the ground below me was too hard. I wanted to build, too—the urge was so strong it hurt my knuckles—but there was nothing to build with. I was standing in a crowd of others like me, and we had nowhere to go.

I felt full. Not the same as when you eat too much or you're backed up, but something was pressing against my insides. It was like nothing I've ever felt awake. What the hell could it be? I could imagine it getting bigger and bigger, like an inflating balloon, until my whole body just burst open. The others' eyes were on me, watching me start to panic, like they understood but they couldn't do anything to help me. *What the hell was it?* This horrible burning, pressing thing?

It didn't matter. I had to open myself and let it out, whatever it was. There was no room to maneuver, to split myself in two, but I had to try. I was terrified the thing would rip me apart as it left my body but more frightened of living with it inside me. More frightened that I wasn't *me* anymore, that—I know this sounds crazy—that *it* was me, and I was going to die if I couldn't get out.

Relief, finally. All of a sudden I felt the thing leave me and the pressure inside disappear. All my muscles went slack. I became hollow as an empty bottle.

The others were watching—impressed, maybe. Or just curious. After a moment, I turned to see what it was I'd birthed. It was brown, oblong, with freckles. An egg.

Crazy thoughts and feelings rushed in to fill all that empty space inside me. *I'm a bird. No! I'm a man! No! I'm a mother. That's me. I'm nuts.* I was proud, I was ashamed, I didn't know what I was.

In the middle of all that, there was this: That egg was the most beautiful thing I've ever seen.

I woke up listening to Dad cough in the next room, and I cried, actually *cried*, into my pillow.

...

Soon as the sun came up, I went out to my bird.

"What the hell is happening?" I yelled at her. She didn't even get up.

"What are you doing to me?" I opened the door of the pen, but she ignored me.

"Hey!" The dream hadn't worn off yet, and now I was worried something was wrong with the bird. I whistled to her. I called her names and tried to lure her out with bread crusts, but she didn't move a muscle.

It hit me: She's brooding.

For a minute, with the dream fresh in my head, I couldn't think what to do. Then I remembered—we'd agreed on a plan, Tommy and me. I phoned him to get him out here. We'd have to collect the eggs and hide them in the semi until Heartfields came and took the birds to slaughter. Then we could clean the barn and wait for the whole thing to start over. There'd be another flock of the Heartfields Cobbs to flush before we could set the eggs out, but I tried not to think about that yet.

While I waited for Tommy, I decided to take my hen's egg. When I went to move her off it, she went wild. I don't know what I was expecting, but not that. She twisted and flapped her way out of my grip, then she attacked me—I mean, really *attacked* me. She was scratching with her spurs and pecking with her beak. I had to kick her twice just to keep her from opening an artery. While she was dazed, I grabbed the egg and got the hell out of there. When I closed up the run behind me, she threw herself down with her wings spread out, screeching like Mom's old opera records. I told her if she didn't stop, I'd have to put her down in the barn like the others.

She didn't stop. So I got my thickest gloves, caged her up, and took her to the barn with me. I couldn't listen to that racket anymore; I just couldn't.

...

Most of the time, the chickens just sat around the barn like blinking pillows, but the minute we tried to take their eggs, the Crosses turned into flapping, scratching demons. We had to work together: I'd grab the bird, and Tommy'd grab the egg.

It took three days to get them all, and we were really racing the clock by the end because the Heartfields trucks showed up just as Tommy was locking the trailer. We came back to the house exhausted and scratched and starving, but when I lay down, I smiled to myself, just thinking about the surprise on the Heartfields guys' faces. We'd filled the trucks to busting—we hadn't lost a bird from this flock, not one.

This check was going to be big, probably our biggest ever. That'd make all the nasty stuff worthwhile, all the work, the scratches, and the lost sleep. We could start paying down our debt again, and I wouldn't have to choose which bills to pay. For the first time in a long time, I thought about the future and it didn't make my stomach shrivel up.

...

In my dream that night, there was no egg. I was hanging upside down—me and the others, all in a line, something pulling us forward by the feet. I wanted to get away, but I couldn't pull myself upright. The smell was disgusting. And, one by one, we passed a blade that sliced our throats open.

I woke up thinking I was choking on my own blood.

Half-awake and coughing, I stumbled past my hamper, down the stairs, and out the back door to the old coop. Taking the eggs and seeing the trucks drive away yesterday—I wanted that to be a dream, too. My bird was in that crowd. If it would have done any good, I would have driven to the plant right then, right to the shining Heartfields complex, to find her.

I found Tommy instead, awake even before me. It was at least an hour to sunrise, but there he was, heading down the driveway. The way I remember it, he had on his button-down shirt and his pressed-front pants, and he was whistling.

I flipped the porch light.

"Joe?" He turned. "What's the matter?"

What did I say? I was furious and desperate, but I didn't know why. I knew we'd sent 20,000 birds to their deaths, but so what? We'd done it before, dozens of times. Hundreds of times. Thousands of birds, millions of birds …

Even without the dreams, I think I would have understood then how you'd hate us.

"Calm down," Tommy said. "Let me get you a drink."

Inside, I let him sit me down. "It was just a bad dream, Joe. You've been thinking about them too much."

I got calmer. What he was saying made sense, and I wanted him to be right. I drank the beer he'd given me, whatever time it was.

"Where were you going?" I asked.

He smiled. "I wanted to be sure I don't miss the check."

Sure, that was why he'd stayed at the house last night. The Heartfields man had never shown up before breakfast, but I thought I understood him. This day we'd find out if all our work had paid off.

I told him to wait. We could all go to the barn together— Dad, too. His lungs would be all right if he took his oxygen and didn't go inside.

Later, as I hosed away litter and loose feathers, I kept an eye out for any eggs we'd missed, but our work was good. From one end, I looked down the whole length of the barn. It was like a football field, yeah, but no turf, no field lights, no excitement. Just concrete under my feet, the food and water pipes, the dark propane lamps overhead. I thought about my hen, how she'd tried to fly around. The ones in here had it even worse. They couldn't even see the sky. They didn't have dirt to dig in, or room to go flapping their wings. I knew what that felt like, because I'd dreamt it.

There were tires on the driveway. Just four tires. Dad and Tommy met the Heartfields man as he stepped out of the pickup with the company logo, holding the two pieces of paper that would decide our future.

"Mr. Jablonsky?" he asked, looking past Dad and Tommy because I was the one he knew. I jogged over, even though I didn't want to. Something was wrong. The trucks should be here with him, carrying the next flock. Without them, that check in his hand was nothing—a stay of execution at best.

"This is your check." The Heartfields man looked at me oddly as he handed it over. Dad and Tommy crowded around, impatient for me to open it. I did it without taking my eyes off the man's face. He held my gaze, too, like he was the one waiting for some explanation—from me, of all people.

Tommy whooped when he saw the amount. Dad pulled it out of my hand and kissed it, then I felt his hands on my back, patting me, congratulating me. Who knows what Tommy was doing—turning cartwheels, probably. I just kept staring at the Heartfields man, waiting for him to accuse us of something.

After a minute, he broke his stare and smoothed the other piece of paper over the hood of his pickup. Then the clicky pen came out. "You need to sign this for the next flock."

"Where are they?" I asked.

"Who?"

"The stock. You ain't got them in your cab, do you?"

The Heartfields man gave me a nervous smile. "I was told you had them here already."

By now Tommy'd come back from his touchdown dance

and he jumped in. "That's right," he said. "They're here already." He took the pen out of the man's hand. "I can sign."

The Heartfields man breathed out, glad he hadn't screwed up. In another minute the deal was done and he was back in his pickup, driving away. I hadn't moved a muscle. The way Dad looked from me to Tommy, with his brow scrunched up, I knew he wasn't in on it.

"Son?" Dad asked. "What's going on?"

"I saved the farm," said Tommy. He smiled and smiled.

...

There's just flashes of what happened after—me shoving Tommy, Tommy clocking me back, me shouting, "How could you?"

Dad got between us and hollered at me to cool down. Then Tommy got to be the bigger man again and said he'd leave for now and explain everything later.

When it was quiet and I was alone and I could think it through, I realized I should have seen it coming. The company was in a death match with the price of chicken what it was, and they had to find any way they could to cut production costs. Just a few cents on the pound mattered, like a few drops of water matters to a man in the desert. The hatchery was always the most expensive part of the business—besides the farming, which they contracted out to chumps like us. With the Phoenix Crosses, Heartfields wouldn't need to keep broody hens anymore.

Our farm was just the first test case. And Tommy had sold them the patent.

He never hated the company. He didn't blame them for the piles of debt, or the uncertainty every eight weeks over what kind of flock we'd get. He didn't care about the lagoons of chicken shit and dead stock, or Dad's cough, or Mom dying. Well, why would he? He had a way out.

And I went along with it, kept it our little secret. Maybe I just wanted us to be a team, like brothers—for a little while, at least.

. . .

I had to get away, and Dad didn't try to stop me.

I got a job driving trucks, hauling anything but chickens. I stopped talking to anyone at home. The only thing I couldn't stop was the dreams. My bird—I think it was her, but in the dream it was me—living her endless lives. Hatching. Growing. Losing her beak. Laying her egg. Dying. Every life was a little bit different, but those parts were the same. It got so I started to know what was coming next, like one of the video games Tommy and me used to play over and over.

Some nights, not even sleeping pills helped.

I knew Dad and Tommy were doing well because Heartfields was doing well. There was a story on TV that talked about the chicken industry, how the Phoenix Crosses were basically a renewable resource—well, at least it meant you didn't need broody hens and hatcheries. Just as soon as a flock went away to slaughter, growers could set the eggs in their barns and incubate the next batch—or hold off, if demand wasn't high enough. The eggs would keep. Hatched, the birds didn't get sick, and the meat tasted great.

Anybody trying to compete with ordinary birds—they were having a hell of a time. Heartfields had just bought up eight more slaughterhouses in eight more towns; they had the national market cornered. International, too, soon enough. And all the credit belonged to Dr. Thomas Jablonsky, Jr., the son of humble chicken farmers. My brother was a hero.

. . .

In my dreams, I was searching my mind for something, like trying to remember a song that I knew a long, long time ago. When I was awake, I wondered what it could be. Something in their phoenix genes? I stared at Tommy's photo of the phoenix on my dashboard, until I was sure.

Tommy and Dad must think I did it, somehow, because it happened the day I came home. Really I was just coming home to warn them.

With the additions Tommy'd put on, the house was twice as big as the one I grew up in, and now Dad had a bedroom and his own bathroom on the ground floor so he didn't have to climb stairs. Upstairs, they'd need the space, Tommy and his new wife. Dad's first grandchild was on the way.

Over beers on the porch, I told Tommy you were learning. The company couldn't keep raising and killing the same birds again and again without a problem. But he didn't believe me, no matter how many times we went around.

"Okay," I said. "Just—just think about it."

"Even if it were true, which it's not," he said, "they're just *birds*, Joe. What are they going to do? They can't even fly."

"I think they have dreams, too," I said. "That means they have minds."

Tommy shook his head. "You're anthropomorphizing."

I shrugged and went back in to get another beer. He followed. When I opened the refrigerator, I saw a single egg, sitting inside a half-dozen carton, and I picked up the whole thing. "What's this?"

Tommy shrugged. "It's good to keep one behind, in case there's a problem. Then I don't have to start from scratch again in the lab."

All at once I thought about my chick, slipping around the plastic hamper. I should have given her someplace better, someplace she could have explored, with a place to perch and somewhere to dig.

Tommy cleared his throat. "I was glad when you called, Joe." He must've gotten used to making deals in our time apart because he didn't sound like a scientist at all anymore. He sounded like a businessman.

"There's so much to do now," he said. "They made me a vice president, and I have to read reports, study other climates." Finally he got to the point. "I thought maybe you'd like to come back, run the farm again."

The egg in my hand suddenly got heavy as a softball, and I nearly dropped it. "I can't work for the company anymore."

"Why not?" he asked.

"Because soon there isn't going to be a company."

...

I meant to at least say good-bye to Dad, but sirens called me and Tommy back outside. From the porch, we could see flames up on the hill, where the Heartfields plant had stood all our lives. For a minute, both of us just stared. What Tommy saw, I can only guess—his future, maybe, going up in a ball of fire and a column of smoke.

I laughed. Finally, they'd remembered the song they wanted, the song to set themselves alight.

Tommy turned like he was going to punch me in the face. "What the hell!"

I ducked and ran. It wasn't until I started the engine of my truck that I realized I still had the egg carton in my hand. Even if I'd had time to plan, though, I'd like to think that I wouldn't have left you behind.

I set the carton down on the seat beside me and took off down the driveway while Tommy hollered and banged on the side of the cab.

I lost him at the road and just drove. For miles and miles, ash coated my windshield as I passed grow-out sheds becoming rows of flame. Sirens on top of sirens blended together like some kind of wailing choir, but under it all, I imagined I could hear birds singing.

I looked to the egg at my right, turned up the heat, and drove on.

For you and me, next time is going to be better.

Shooting a Mule

J. Bowers

Fie. 1.—INSTANTANEOUS PHOTOGRAPHY—BEFORE THE EXPLOSION

"It became necessary, one day, at Willet's Point, to destroy a worthless mule, and the subject was made the occasion of giving useful instruction to the military class there stationed."
—*Scientific American*, September 24, 1881

DICKY KEEPS SAYING that things could have gone differently if that damned fool mule had had the good sense not to cow-kick General Abbot in the thigh this Thursday last. A barrel of salt pork could easily have been pressed into service, or a side of rotting beef, but no, that rotten mule had to go and assault a commanding officer, and so, Dicky reckoned, he had to pay.

"See, a *horse* would have shown some respect," he said, crooking his mouth to spit. "But once you start putting donkey in there, it's just *unnatural*, the creature's instincts get all mixed up, it starts getting its own ideas about who's boss, against God's plan, and I tell you what, that's a dangerous thing." He ground his spit into the ruddy dirt with his boot heel and nodded vigorously as he reached for his snuff. "It'll get just what it deserves, and I tell you, I'm sure going to watch."

He was. But then, we all were. General Abbot's vendetta against "Colonel," the mid-aged grade mule that had left him with a bruise shaped like a cannonball, was already the stuff of legend around our battalion, and the General's revenge was, if Dicky's account of the matter was to be believed, destined for epic scale. The General was a ruthless man at best, and the old Colonel's assault, prompted by a cinch pulled too tight, had invoked the General's purest wrath. That afternoon, he submitted us to hours of calisthenics under the New York summer sun. He trampled the already suffering scrub grass of the parade ground, all the while slapping a riding crop against his bad thigh, as if to prolong the pain and, through it, stoke the steaming engine of his rage.

By evening, during an impromptu dinner party at Corporal Smith's palatial manse, the beast's fate was sealed. The execution was imminent, and the secret method employed would, we heard, be a modern wonder worthy of Barnum himself, a spectacular of American know-how. Dicky began collecting bets at sundown, weighing the odds of electrocution versus firing squad, his eyes two thin slits in his leathern face as Henry, Thom, and all my chums invented novel ways to die.

But even the condemned should receive last rites. And that, it seemed, was left to me. I stole from my bed in the pitch of night, while my bunkmates snored on, unaware. I made my way to the stable softly. The horses were whales in the dark, silently shifting through the black, their massive bodies drifting just above the earth as they cropped the dewy brown grass. Not a soul was in sight, save them. And I was frightened as one is frightened in church. I, who had thrown rocks at them mere days before, drunk on cider with Dicky and Thom.

The mule I found alone, sequestered in a round pen beside the main barn, his great bullish head butting up against an empty feed drum, his huge brown eyes limpid, innocent of the drama that now surrounded him. He greedily lipped the handfuls of grass that I pushed through the fence and allowed me to groom the long black funnels of his ears, stretching his neck out so I could scratch them. We smoked my last pipe of Cavendish together, that mule and I. And he seemed glad for the companionship of a fellow creature, however unfamiliar, his damp nostrils flaring and huffing, his warm breath joining coils of smoke.

As reveille sounded next morning, we were visited by the General himself. He marched through our bunkhouse, a wide grin slashing his bearded face, his best riding crop beating a tattoo upon his massive right thigh. A mincing, suited businessman brought up the rear, his shoulders burdened with an array of leather satchels, his forehead slick with perspiration despite the chill of the room. We dressed with rapidity and scrambled to attention.

"Today, boys, you will bear witness to history," announced General Abbot, his crop thwacking the footboard of Dicky's bed so hard the metal rang out. My bowels crept at the sound. "With the technological assistance of my new acquaintance, this Englishman, Mr. Charles Bennett, I shall perform a grand experiment in the new art of"—and here the General looked to Bennett, who prompted him with a wormlike twist of the lips—"*instantaneous photography*, the likes of which the world has never known, and never shall again."

We were forthwith trooped out of the bunkhouse, unwashed and unbreakfasted, to a barren tract of land just south of the parade ground. There stood the Colonel, motionless and trusting, his rope tied securely to a wooden stake freshly driven into the earth. A makeshift surcingle secured around his girth was, we saw, elaborately attached to a host of electrical wires running through the dirt.

Upon our arrival, Bennett immediately rushed toward a tripod that straddled the land like a strange metal insect. The General boldly strode toward a card table ranged approximately thirty feet away from the beast, and we followed like puppies, jostling one another to take our places on either side of him, hastily buttoning our jackets and trousers. The table held a gadget I'd never seen before, and the General stood with one hand on either side of it, as if protecting the mysterious machinery from our prying eyes. We watched, puzzled, as Bennett approached the animal, accompanied by a petty officer who gentled it with a whiff of ether whilst a necklace of wire and gunnysacks was fastened about its noble neck. The daguerreotypist spoke then, his accent clipped and purposeful.

"The experiment will proceed as follows. The slide of my camera is supported by a fuse; this fuse and the payload attached to the subject are connected in the same electrical circuit, arranged by my assistant. On General Abbot's signal, an electrical pulse shall travel through the wiring, simultaneously activating the explosives and dropping my camera's slide, capturing the very second of detonation on one of my patented Instantaneous Gelatine Photographic Plates for all posterity."

The mule's vast ears flicked toward the sound of Bennett's voice, then toward Dicky, who was the first to applaud. And I stood at war with myself, scarcely believing where I was, the plain words "explosives" and "payload" ringing in my ears. The fear that the mule knew by scent that I, too, was here, complicit in its killing, bridled against years of conditioning to remain behind the card table, shoulders back, chin up, until ordered otherwise. But then—

"Fire!" shouted the General, his hammy hands slamming down upon the device in front of him. And in a terrible instant, head was ejected from body, its momentary flight filling the air with a bloody mist until both portions of the animal fell to the ground, still. The General strode jauntily toward the steaming carcass, first lifting the beast's belly with the toe of his boot, then, with a broad smile, doffing his hat in the direction of the triumphant daguerreotypist, who excitedly exclaimed that, since all his equipment had worked as planned, we could soon expect him to publish an image of the headless creature, still standing, before the body had time to fall.

That evening, over cigars, Dicky declared the whole affair a delicious success, great sport, and supremely edifying for all involved, particularly the mule. He said he couldn't wait for the photograph.

Later, silent in my bunk, I wondered if he and I had seen the same thing.

Images courtesy of David L. Spahr, stereoviews.com

Lost Pets

Laura Maylene Walter

THE LOST-PET SIGNS appear on every telephone pole along Barnard Street, which dead-ends into the park. It's not much of a park, just a scrub of land shaped like a baseball diamond with some trees, a small basketball court, and a jungle gym no kids ever play on. For some reason, people are convinced their lost cats and dogs gather here, maybe in the middle of the night under the moon.

I have a good view of the moon tonight from my bedroom window. My neighbor Joshua across the street is up late; I can tell by the single patch of light in his third-floor window. I wonder what he does up there by himself at this time of night. Maybe he's like me and can't sleep. Maybe he also wonders where the pets go, and maybe he peeks through his window to catch sight of a phantom cat dashing across the park. In the process he might glance this way and see me pressed against the curtains of my bedroom window, gazing out at the pale glow of stars.

...

LACY has gone missing. Big fat tabby with long whiskers. Please call day or night.

We had a dog when I was growing up. His name was Scooter, and he had bad hips. But that was when he was old. When he was young, he'd dash through the park after the Frisbee and bring it back, over and over. That's what my mother told me, anyway. I was too young to remember Scooter like that. For me, he was always the dog with the gray around his muzzle who let me play with the silky underside of his ear and who sighed when he eased himself onto the floor.

Back then my mother would stand on the porch and shield her eyes against the sun, looking for Scooter in the distance. She was always afraid he would run away. "Lord help me if the day comes," she'd say and shake his red leash into the air. "Lord help me, Scooter, come back!"

He always did.

...

LOST DOG Starlight. Very affectionate, friendly with strangers. Mutt, all brown with white back left foot. Our son misses her dearly.

Every time I pass a lost-pet poster on my street or in the park, I let a wave of pity roll through my body and then I keep walking. I'm like anybody else: I glance at the poster, I frown, but I don't for a second consider looking for the animal. I know better.

Then I find the poster for Starlight, a brown, medium-sized dog that looks like Scooter. I see it in the photocopied black eyes, the way they stare out at me from the flyer stapled to the pole outside my house. Before I stop to think, I tear the poster down. I stuff it in my pocket and dash back into my house, where I un-crumple the paper and tape it to the bedroom wall. I sit on my bed a long time and look at it. My bed is a water bed, so I sway a bit as I sit.

I remember the day my mother told me about Scooter. She was picking me up from school and waited until I climbed in the back seat of the minivan. She didn't pull away from the curb after I was buckled in, and this was how I knew something was wrong. "Scooter died," she said. She waited. "Did you hear me? He's dead. I found him lying on the kitchen floor." She started to cry, but I stayed quiet. I was seven years old. I didn't cry for Scooter then, and I didn't cry for him later. I was too busy creating an alternate ending for him: Instead of dying, he ran away. He wasn't gone, just lost, and would surely make it home when we needed him most.

The light drifting through my window grows weaker, but I don't move. I stay on the bed and stare at the lost-dog notice until I'm entirely in the dark.

...

TRIXIE. Male Shih Tzu mix. Can sit, lie down, heel on command. Trixie is new to the neighborhood and may have lost his way.

In the park the next day, I'm taking down a poster for Trixie, a little white yippy dog—that's what my mother would have called it—when someone taps me on the shoulder, making me jump.

"What are you doing?"

It's Joshua. He's wearing a dark-gray coat and a blue-and-white striped scarf. The way the wool gathers around his neck fills me with despair. Or desire. I don't know if I can tell the difference anymore.

I step back from the poster, leaving it half-attached to the pole. "I thought I saw this dog," I tell him. The upper corner of the paper curls over, covering the little dog's face.

"Really?" He steps forward. "Where?" His hands have come out of his jacket pockets, and he looks half a step away from grabbing me.

"Well. My house is that one, over there? I thought I saw a little white dog run through my backyard this morning." I'd taken my coffee on the back porch and had spent a good ten minutes staring at the clouds, those little white puffs. Close enough.

"That's my dog," Joshua says. "I live across the street."

"I know. We met at that Fourth of July thing."

"Oh."

"Vicky," I remind him. "We talked about artificial popcorn flavoring. You have a cousin or something who got that popcorn lung disease."

"You have a good memory."

"Did she decide to sue?"

Joshua shakes his head. "I don't know. Look, about my dog. Which direction did he run?"

"Um. Across the park?"

"You sure?" He looks at me closely, and this time he does reach out to put a hand on my shoulder. "Will you help me look for him?"

"He's a boy and his name is Trixie?"

"My son named him."

"You have a son *and* a dog?" I don't see how this is possible, considering all the time I spend at my window.

"I'd really appreciate some help."

"Of course," I say, and we cross the park together. We don't speak for many steps. A lost-cat notice blows across the grass in front of me. Sometimes Joshua glances my way and I point halfheartedly at Trixie's supposed path. I wonder how long this will last, how far we will go—can I make him walk all the way across town?

We circle the park three times and finally take a cold seat on the jungle gym. I try to bait him with a few questions, testing to see if he remembers our conversation from last summer. I had told him the truth then, about my career as an engineer, and about how my father died when I was young. But Joshua seems to be thinking only of his dog. Our breath forms clouds in the sky. It's like breathing out little Trixies.

"I'll get my car," Joshua says finally. "I'll start in the direction you saw him run."

So he still believes me.

. . .

LOST. Beans, small black female, spayed, has all claws and not afraid to use them.

My lost-pet collection grows to include signs for six cats and nine dogs. I tape the flyers one by one onto my bedroom wall, with Starlight in the middle. It says right there that Starlight's back left foot is white. Scooter didn't have any white markings, on his feet or elsewhere. Still, I look at Starlight and think, *You are Scooter.* I wish I could call my mother and tell her that I had been right about Scooter only being lost. We could ignore the passing of all these improbable years to focus on the very real and very found dog sitting before us. But most likely I'll settle for calling Joshua instead, later in the night after his light blinks off. That's when I want to catch him, when he's breathing into the dark.

The first time Joshua comes over for dinner and doesn't leave right after dessert, I wonder if he'll kiss me. I wonder if he might want to go upstairs.

"I'm painting my bedroom," I tell him. This is the cleverest plan I can come up with. "So it's a mess up there right now, but soon it will be sea-foam green. Very calming."

He doesn't care. He just refills my wineglass and, on his way back from the kitchen, stops to look through my CD collection.

"It's so quiet," he says.

I laugh. "I don't have kids, I don't have dogs. Nice, huh?"

He looks at me funny. I file this moment away, yet another thing I must learn.

"It's just," I add, "you live right across the street, and I never knew you had a dog. Isn't that strange? You'd think I would have noticed you walking it or something."

"I only got Trixie a few weeks ago."

"Still. It's funny, isn't it, how two people can live in such close proximity and know nothing about each other?"

"We know something now."

"Maybe," I say. He edges closer on the couch and I shut up, fast. It's been a long time since I had a boyfriend, too long, and just having Joshua next to me on this worn sofa with the stretched-out slipcover makes me want to hold my breath. So I do, and I close my eyes and wait for him to lean in for a kiss. I wait and I wait. Finally, I open my eyes to find he's not on the couch anymore; he's gotten up and has gone to stand by the window. The room is still. I decide he's right, that my house is too quiet. I need something to fill it.

That night, after Joshua has left, I return to my pet posters. I start from the upper left corner and work around the perimeter. I always return to Starlight in the middle. She looks out at me, her head tilted slightly to the left, her expression poised and passive and entirely lost.

A faint sound from the street carries up through my bedroom window. I part the curtains. A woman is there on the sidewalk, stapling a piece of paper to the telephone pole. A little girl in a pink coat stands next to her, crying.

. . .

LOST. MY NAME IS MALCOLM. I AM A MALE TABBY, 2 YEARS OLD. ON SEPT 26, I DECIDED TO WANDER OFF FROM MY HOME AT 548-1 ALBERTS STREET. PLEASE FIND ME AND CALL MY OWNER.

I decide to call the numbers on the flyers. I start with the cat poster the little girl and her mother put up last night, and then I call the others, everyone except Starlight's family and Joshua. I dial, listen to the voice and the breath on the other end, and then I hang up. Whenever someone doesn't answer, I think, *See how careless you're being? See?* They should have answered, just in case.

Joshua has his son this weekend. I have to spy on them from my bedroom window because Joshua has decided not to introduce me to Colin yet. We need to give it time, Joshua said. But from here I watch Colin wander around the front yard. He carries a big stick and stops periodically to wave it like a flag or a threat. He slashes the air as if he's carrying a sword, and then he looks straight up into my window.

We make eye contact. I raise my hand, as if I'm about to be sworn in. Colin squints, shakes his head, and turns away. Beats at the grass with the stick.

I turn from the window and face my wall of pets. Trixie's little white face is pasted to the bottom right corner. Joshua only has Colin one weekend a month, so I can see how I missed him. But why hadn't I noticed Trixie?

Maybe I can only see the pets who are already gone.

. . .

ALL IS LOST. MR. CHIPMUNK, $100 REWARD.
On Saturday, I stroll through the park to check the

posters, but none of them are new. Lacy, Beans, Malcolm, Mr. Chipmunk. The grass under my feet is short and grayish, as if the green has leaked out.

As I pass the jungle gym and head toward the basketball court, I hear distant barking that slowly grows louder. A medium-sized brown dog appears far off by the tree line and hurries in my direction, her tail flapping like a helicopter propeller. She comes closer and closer and slides to a stop at my feet. I hold out my hand, which she sniffs. She's not wearing a collar.

"Hello, Starlight," I say. She hesitates and finally, slowly, starts to wag her tail.

She follows me home and right into the house. In the kitchen, she turns in three circles and sniffs the linoleum. I fill a ceramic mixing bowl with water and put it on the floor. Then I go up to my bedroom, pull down the poster, and bring it back down the stairs.

I hold the paper right next to the dog's face. Starlight develops a nervous air, like she's auditioning for something. I peer closer at the poster, then at the dog, until I remember the white paw. At first I think it's a bust, but then I reach down and rub the dust from her feet. She lets me. I reveal a white patch on her foot.

"Well," I say to Starlight. "I guess that's it."

We stare at each other. Starlight yawns and curls up for a nap. Only then do I grab my jacket and race through the neighborhood to rip down every Starlight flyer I can find.

...

LOST CAT. Diamond, all black with two white front paws. No collar. She's an indoor cat and it's a mystery how she escaped.

"Where'd you get the dog?" Joshua asks.

I'm making dinner, vegetarian chili. The cornbread comes from a boxed mix, but I hid the box in the trash before Joshua came over.

"The shelter." I peer into the chili pot. Its contents bubble back at me.

Joshua has bent to scratch behind Starlight's ears. "What's her name?"

"Scooter."

"Isn't she a girl?"

I salt the chili. "You're the one with a male dog named Trixie."

Joshua is frowning at Starlight. "I feel like I've seen her before."

"You know what they say. All dogs look alike."

"No one says that."

I shrug.

"So you got her at the shelter," he says, then stops as if he has to mull this over for a while.

"Yep." I pull the pan of cornbread out of the oven. It smells amazing. Starlight comes over to rub against me. At first I think she's being affectionate, but then I realize she's trembling, just a little, just enough to feel against my leg. She's looking blankly in the distance, like she's remembering something. I reach down and pat her head, trying to bring her attention back in the room. Joshua watches.

"I wonder if Trixie will ever come back," he says.

I leave Starlight and set a steaming bowl of chili on the table in front of Joshua. *No*, I think. *Not a chance.*

. . .

LOST DOG I THINK MY EX-HUSBAND MIGHT HAVE

STOLE HER IF YOU SEE THIS DOG OR KURT FRANKLIN CALL ME IMMEDIATELY DAY OR NITE.

Starlight sits obediently at my feet. In a few minutes, her tail will start to flip lightly against the floor. She's smart. It's been less than a week, and already she knows when I will take her for a walk. We'll stroll to the other end of Barnard and then back, and then we'll go through the park and I'll throw the tennis ball. I have to be careful, though, and stick to the protection of the trees so no one will spot us, and even then I only let her off the leash for short stretches. She still gets that faraway look sometimes, like she's listening to something my human ears can't hear.

After our walk, I put the teakettle on the stove and drop a biscuit into Starlight's bowl. I'm humming along to the radio. Starlight clicks up and down the linoleum. I look at her skinny toes and think that winter will be here sooner than later. Maybe I'll learn to knit.

The doorbell rings. I wipe my hands on the dish towel and head to the front door, where I find Joshua standing slouched at the shoulders with his hands in his pockets.

"Can I come in?"

"Of course." I stand back but frown a little, behind his back. He's pacing in my front hallway. Starlight comes bounding in to greet him, and then she follows his pacing, stride for stride.

"Come into the kitchen. I'm making tea."

Joshua thrusts his hand into his jacket pocket and pulls out a crumpled piece of paper. "Are you sure the shelter held Scooter long enough?"

"What are you talking about?" I make a point of not looking at the paper in his hands.

"The shelter holds lost dogs for a little while, to see if someone claims them. I think they let Scooter go too early." He holds the paper out and, with shaking fingers, I take it. It's

Starlight's poster. I hold it tightly in my hands, the very same picture tacked up to my bedroom wall.

"This isn't Scooter," I say. "Can't you tell by the face? Totally different dog."

Joshua snatches the paper back. "Look," he says, and holds it up to Starlight.

"The shelter people told me this dog had been there for weeks and weeks. They were just about to put her down."

Joshua is crouched by Starlight, staring from the dog to the paper, back and forth. "It's the same dog. Can't you see? It's obvious."

I go to the fridge and grab a beer, the lager Joshua likes, and pop it open with my art deco bottle opener. I put a smile on my face and hold it out to him.

"Here, drink this. You'll feel better."

Joshua looks up at me as if I'm crazy. He's still crouched by Starlight with that damn poster. I put my hand on his shoulder, where I can feel the muscles under his shirt. The beer is sweating against my other hand.

"I know what's going on here," I tell him, making my voice soothing. "You're so worried about Trixie that you think bringing back someone else's dog will make you feel better. But this is Scooter, Joshua." I remove my hand from his shoulder to gesture to the dog. "And Scooter is mine now."

Joshua doesn't take the beer. Starlight moves away from both of us and goes to the back door. She doesn't whine to go out but instead just stares at the door vacantly, as though if she concentrates hard enough, I'll open it to reveal her previous life.

"This dog," Joshua says slowly, "is Starlight. You need to call this number." He's looking down at Scooter and refuses to meet my eyes. "Sometimes I wonder if you ever saw Trixie at all."

"Of course I saw Trixie. I saw him run through the park,

just like I said. Why would I make that up?"

Joshua turns to face me. "Then what?"

I frown. "What do you mean?"

"What happened after you saw Trixie? Did you take him home, just like you took Starlight?"

"Don't be crazy. You need a drink. Don't you want a drink?" The beer is ice in my hand. "Maybe I should open some wine."

"I don't want anything." Joshua turns and wanders down the hallway, toward the staircase. Starlight snaps out of her trance and follows, trying to grab her own poster with her teeth. I put the beer down and trail behind them. Joshua pauses in the foyer for a moment, as if he's deep in thought. At one point, his hand lands on the staircase banister, and he glances up. Instinctively, I move in front of the staircase and hold out my arms.

"I told you. The bedroom's being renovated," I say.

"You said you were painting, not renovating."

"Same thing."

He takes a step closer. When he speaks, his voice is very low, so low he doesn't sound like himself anymore. "I know you look out at my house sometimes. I see you in the window, behind the curtains."

"I never took you for the paranoid type." I reach for the poster, but he snatches it away from me.

"You're hiding something." He glances around again, searching. "Trixie's up there, isn't he?"

"Don't be ridiculous."

"I want to see that bedroom."

"Joshua. Have some decency." I try to block the stairs again, but he simply lowers my arm and starts up the staircase without me. Starlight bounds along beside him, her feet clicking on the wooden stairs, and I have no option but to follow.

Joshua first peeks in the bathroom and then the empty spare room before finding my bedroom. He lets himself in while Starlight runs behind him, twirling in circles and barking manically. I creep toward the doorway and lean against the wall, waiting.

"Jesus," Joshua says. He's standing in front of the wall of pet posters. By now I have nine dogs and ten cats. Starlight in the middle, of course, but the first thing Joshua notices is Trixie. He rips the flyer off the wall and waves it at me. "What the hell?"

"It's just a collection. Some people collect stamps or coins. This is cheaper." I try to smile but can't quite make it.

"So you never saw Trixie at all."

"How do I know you're not the one lying to me? Maybe you saw me looking at that flyer and pretended he was yours to get me to talk to you." As the words come out of my mouth, I start to believe them. It's kind of clever, actually. I wish I'd thought of it earlier, whenever I saw a good-looking guy standing near a lost-pet sign on the café bulletin board.

Joshua finally registers Starlight's poster in the middle. "Well, shit. You stole someone's dog."

"*Stole* is a strong word. Look, she loves me." I call to Starlight, and she trots over, her tongue lolling out of her mouth. At least it's not Trixie, I think. Maybe that will be enough to save me.

He rattles the poster in his hands. "If you don't call these people, I will."

"Josh. Please."

He raises his head and looks at me, clear-eyed. "I can't believe this whole time I lived across the street from someone like you."

. . .

BLACK CAT. Hello, this is a photo of our cat, but he's not actually lost. He died and I didn't know how to break it to my 3-year-old daughter, so I said he ran away. She insisted we try to find the cat so I made up these posters. Don't judge, this is out of love.

I find this flyer the next day, clear across town where I bring Starlight for a walk by the railroad tracks. From a distance I could tell it's a poster I don't have yet. At first I'm excited to have a new one, then ashamed when I remember my fight with Joshua, and finally conflicted when I actually read it. I consider taking the poster down and adding it to my collection, but I stop myself at the last minute. It's not real, and it doesn't count. That cat is not lost somewhere in the world like the others.

It's like that long-ago time I made posters for Scooter in my crooked child's handwriting. They were meant to be a secret, but I couldn't resist tacking them up around the neighborhood. When my mother found out, she brought the posters to me and laid them down in a row on the living room carpet. She looked straight at me but didn't say a word.

I bend over at the waist and take a deep, ragged breath. Starlight gives my face a few nervous licks. I let her. When I'm able to stand up again, I turn away from the cat poster and wipe the tears from my face. Starlight circles at my feet, panting lightly. She's looking into the distance again, her body tensed and ready to run. I left my cell phone at home, not that it matters, because the only person I'd want to call is my mother so she could tell me what it was like when Scooter died. How she handled it, how she dealt with this pain. What it felt to be truly on her own at last. Scooter was just a dog, but he was her life. With him, she wasn't alone.

My mother tried to tell me about pet heaven after Scooter died, but she cried the whole time, and I couldn't bring myself to believe, not even at that young age. Anyone could tell by looking in her face that it just wasn't true. And so I pictured instead a loose Scooter running free.

With Starlight still prancing around my legs, I sit down heavily on the curb. All at once, I want to believe in pet heaven. I want to think that all these lost animals end up in a place where they never grow tired or get in fights or go hungry. They take sun-drenched naps and wake snuggled together, warm, their hearts beating close enough to remind them of their mothers.

"Come here, Scooter," I say and stroke her silky ears. She stays still for this, almost too still, as if she can make up for what I have lost if only she is good enough.

...

STILL MISSING. $500 REWARD FOR STARLIGHT'S SAFE RETURN.

The new flyer appears that evening. I stare at it for a long time, that dollar amount, and then glance around, as if someone might be watching. I rip the flyer off the pole in one quick motion and hurry back home.

I could hide Starlight for a while, maybe with my friend Karen in Ohio. Or I could disguise her, maybe dye her fur? Turn that back foot from white to black? My mother would have liked that. She would have encouraged anything that let me keep this dog, I just know it. I need to think of a better plan.

Or I could call that number and return Starlight to her family.

Starlight's new poster says she has a nine-year-old boy waiting at home. The parents had him add, "Please help find my best friend," in his own handwriting at the bottom. That was kind of genius. That's the reason I'm hovering over my cell phone, about to pick it up.

But I'm not sure. Maybe Joshua is too cowardly to turn me in. Besides, that back paw isn't all white. Just partially. And who could tell if these are really Starlight's eyes when the poster's such a bad photocopy? This could be anyone's dog. It could be no one's. It could be mine.

I hold the poster in my left hand and pick up the phone with my right. I don't have to do this. Starlight lies contentedly at my feet. She'll fall asleep soon, then twitch mid-dream. I sigh and dial the number on the sheet. It rings once, twice. When someone finally answers I close my eyes. I can't speak.

"Hello?" the voice on the other end says. "Hello? Anyone there?" I bet she hasn't hung up yet in case it's about Starlight. It's been weeks, and still they're hoping.

I open my eyes, ready to speak, when Starlight sits up to study me. I look at her but think instead of Joshua. Then I blink and everything shifts, and I'm seeing my mother, way back when she shook Scooter's leash into the air. It hurts, it's paralyzing, and that woman on the phone is breathing into my ear, but I'm not talking.

Starlight bumps her cold nose along the back of my hand, and when I look into her eyes I see the glossy reflection of something hard to translate, some inscrutable combination of freedom and longing. She sits on her narrow haunches and looks at me, waiting, trusting that she'll be granted a return to her past life. For a moment, I think I understand where pets go when they disappear, and why we are left behind, clumsy and grieving and lost, unable to follow.

The woman has started asking, "Are you there? Are you there?" over and over. I hang up and tuck the phone in my pocket. Within seconds, I feel the vibrations of an incoming call, but I ignore it. I call Starlight's name and she thrusts her snout in my hands. I pet her all over. I speak in low tones and soothe her shivering. I treat her like my own.

Exotic Animal Alert: Please Post Widely

Ramola D

WHEN THE STORY CAME OUT, we learned how time had passed in the life of this leopard—how, never knowing freedom of any kind for eleven years, he had still developed a taste for it when he escaped, then eluded capture for three weeks. We knew Ray Mertens held wild animals. Not just the ones he kept in that zoo of his, with mountain lions and capuchin monkeys and black panthers, right in the middle of Gretchen, Illinois, which people were fooled by. (Just because you could see corn growing in the fields and cattails in the swamp and redbirds flying by, mothers with young children thought nothing of going right up to the cages and sticking their hands in and trying to pet the brutes. They must have thought it was a petting zoo. They stopped that, all right, after that man whose child's arm got torn off tried to tussle with the albino Bengal tiger, and his elbow got ripped and his head smashed and clawed to bits, but Ray Mertens—he didn't stop anything.) After all those citations and fines and such, he just kept on going with the zoo, and he kept some of the creatures in his house, too. This leopard was one of those, a six-foot-long animal, and he kept him in a cage fit for a dog; he could barely turn around.

I visited them once; Ray's wife, Janet, had joined our gardening club (she grew peonies). The leopard was in the family room in a metal cage on a wooden platform on wheels, just off the kitchen, and near a window with the blinds high so he could see out, just like a domestic cat.

It's a shock to anyone to see an animal like that in a cage inside a house, and I admit freely I was afraid. We're not talking a Siamese cat here, or a cute little Pomeranian, or even a blue-eyed pit bull. This was a full-grown, wild leopard—claws, teeth, fangs.

When I first saw him—those yellow eyes were depthless, lakes he could pull you into and drown you in, without conscience—I tell you, it sent a shiver through me, from the top of my head down to my toes. There was a fetid scent in the room, a kind of musky, wet-hide smell mixed in with odors I can only describe as raw meat or stale feces. It came in a wall of smell toward me and made me doubly afraid. I didn't want to go in there—it was hardly believable—but that's where Janet was sitting, right there on her couch, next to the cage, watching some old rerun of *Little House on the Prairie*.

I stood in the doorway first and shot questions at her. Like, "Is that door locked? Is it safe to come in there? Is he likely to come out? What do you do if he escapes?" She just laughed and said, "It's very safe, my dear. I wouldn't be sitting here if that door was not tightly shut and locked."

So I came slowly into the room and sat beside her, on

the far side of the cage, closer to the door, and I gave her my packets of seeds—nasturtiums, zinnias, green echinacea—and she talked about peonies, how you feed them in spring and mulch them and cosset them, one year to the next. And all the while, this yellowish-black spotted leopard—a clouded leopard, she said he's called—stared at us, head on his paws, lying down and staring through the cage at us, with no expression at all.

. . .

He sees faces on top of bodies, held upright. He sees eyes in which fear rocks like a bruise. He has been here so long his muscles feel soft, like the chicken flesh he eats, warped to the rough sawdust surface of the metal cave in which he lies, cave with bars from which there is no refuge, the open, barred cave. Exposed in this fashion, day in, day out.

His eyes search her eyes, the newcomer's eyes. Instinctively he probes. Smelling the fear, sharp smell of panic loosened from cells and diffused in wide concentric rings toward him, sensing the rising want inside himself to charge forward.

The dream of nighttime freedom once more swells against his mind.

In that glistening nighttime world when these bars melt away, the room melts away, the wall melts away, and moonlight glistens all over the black leaf-ridden floor of forest, what is there to prevent him?

. . .

No one really talked to Ray and Janet Mertens at first, not in the town. They lived way out there in the middle of corn and soybean fields, past that stand of woods by the redbird swamp, and only the zoo-goers went there, down that rickety path by the tulip woods, following those wooden signs for UNUSUAL CREATURE ZOO RETREAT, coming out in their pickups and SUVs and Chevrolets from the towns around us. Ray and Janet shopped at the Food Star, sure, and he was in and out of Wick's Hardware, Lowe's even, but the group of us women who ran the Fourth of July and Harvest festivals and dressed up the ruins of the old civic center in the center of town for Halloween didn't know the first thing about Janet Mertens. What we knew was what we saw: They had started a zoo, highly unusual for this part of the world, but there it was. They bought the land, built the fences, carted the cages in on big semi trucks, set up the signs—and people started coming. They brought some business to the town, and some employment for the handlers—all that was nice and all, but the Collinses, whose dairy farm was the closest to them on the south side, and the Turners, whose apple orchard was nearer on their east side, both said they didn't like it.

If you had animals like that—wild cats from the Amazon and crazy, howling monkeys from Africa and who knows what else—there was always the chance one of them would break out of his cage one day, when he was being fed, maybe, or his cage being cleaned, and make a run for it.

And that leopard in the house. It makes you wonder what kind of people they are. Where did that leopard come from? When Janet Mertens showed up at the gardening club last summer, holding her giant fuchsia and antique rose peonies in one hand and a fresh-baked cherry pie in the other, we were hard-pressed not to take her in. We had to, of course—we're all Christian families here, but underneath the face of our politeness, you could see all the little wheels of our minds churning and grinding like teeth, wanting to take chunks out of her.

...

When I visited the Mertens' household that time, I'd gone only because Janet called and told me she had twisted her ankle and she couldn't come to the meeting that month—did I want to come out and bring her some seeds? She said she would show me how she grew her peonies. I went because somebody had to, and I happened to be president of the club that year.

The room felt claustrophobic. It was full of clutter—magazines and newspapers on the coffee table, cabinets filled with plates and cups and funny ceramic figures. All around her—in wooden shelves nailed to the wall, on the tops of bookcases and the mantel over the fireplace—were these tiny ceramic figures, of little fat men and dwarves, spotted red-and-white mushrooms, blue-clad shepherdesses, women acrobats in scanty attire swinging from trapezes, three-dimensional shamrocks, all sorts of bulbous, glossy, oddly shaped things.

It was distracting, but I asked about the leopard, and she twisted her head and looked at him fondly and said, "Oh, yes, Sokar, we've had him since he was a child." Just like that, as if it were normal to refer to a leopard as a child, or keep one in a cage beside you all his life.

"And does he come out and play?" I ventured to ask, and she turned to me with a look of quite serious consternation on her face, as if I had overlooked something fairly basic. She said, "My dear, whatever do you mean? He is a wild animal! He has to be caged!" We both stared at each other then, mutually at a loss.

I had been waiting for some long story to unfold, some saga of I don't know what—love or obsession, maybe, fascination with leopards, a companion since childhood, and she told me nothing. I wanted to ask, *Why do you keep him then? Doesn't he belong in the wild?* But those round eyes of hers kept looking into mine, and a muscle by her mouth was twitching. I felt sorry for her. She was almost sixty-five years old, her hair was all straggly and white, and she was hunched over with all the weight she carried, as if the two parts of her body wanted to reach toward each other, protect her center. She had no children.

Her husband, whom I'd met briefly as I turned into their driveway—a large, striking-looking man with his shock of white hair and piercing blue eyes, a square white moustache obscuring his mouth—had grunted when I spoke to him. He looked taciturn and unsociable. I wondered if he talked to her. I wondered how they had met, whether this was a second marriage or a third. I wondered many things, but I voiced none of them.

She got up and hobbled into the kitchen, made us tea, took out some macadamia-nut cookies from a tin, and told me a little of their life. They used to be circus people, she said, in the old days, when Ray made the lions leap through the Ring of Fire and the tigers sit on tiny stools. They had left because Ray had problems with the management. He spoke his mind, she said, and that had not gone down well. They worked in a zoo afterwards, then a breeding facility for the zoos. That was how they met Sokar.

His father was an old zoo leopard, from India. His mother was a new zoo capture, also from India—a ferocious creature, she said, always rattling her cage and banging her head against the bars. She'd been taken by the Assam Zoo after forest officials captured her; she had attacked villagers up in the mountains, and there was a price on her head. But he, Sokar, had been born in a cage, lived his entire life in a cage. He would know nothing of any other life, she said. His whole experience was captivity.

I looked through the kitchen door at him then. He was standing up in his cage, tail swaying a little, eyes fixed on a bird at the birdfeeder she had hung just outside the window. The bird was making cheeping sounds, and he was looking hungrily at it.

...

The knowing of what it is to steal up behind such a one as him—bird or mouse or slithering snake—ambush in the dark, when he least expected it.

The wanting to leap—coil and spring, rise in a passioned rush—the wanting to tear feathers from the throat, rip tail to a shower of quills, sink teeth into the pulsing soft body of him.

One especially he wishes to sink teeth into, tear apart limb to limb.

Him of the sticks and shouts, him of the constant rage.

Him of the eyes that fix and burn. Him of the cleaning sticks and feeding sticks and beating sticks. Him of the frantic, spraying hose. The one he grew up with. He comes into the room, stands there; his need fills up the room.

...

She showed me pictures then, of herself and her husband in their younger days. She was wearing a gymnast's costume in shiny, pale colors, a tiara holding her gleaming gold hair back; she was upside down on a horse; she was swinging from a trapeze; she was walking on her hands. And him—tall, young, dapper, a long stick in one hand, a streaming white scarf in the other. He was leaping between lions, waving them through flaming circles of fire, balancing on an elephant's back, wearing an expression of ferocity. He was fencing with a cub, a small leopard cub, inside a cage, a long stick in his hand, to which the cub clung with his teeth, forepaws up.

At first he tried to train Sokar for the circus, Janet said, since the circus bought him. But Sokar refused to listen; he didn't take to the training. It was a dead loss to the circus. It made Ray upset.

I could see the upset in his face in the photos of him as he leapt at the cub and the cub leapt up at the stick, as he swung the cub around on the stick and slammed shut the cage's door.

"He almost killed the cub," said Janet, "trying to train him. He wouldn't let a leopard cub beat him. But I talked him into putting him in our zoo instead."

"So he's part of the zoo then?" I was puzzled because the animal was in the house with them.

"Once he was. But there's something between Ray and that animal."

I didn't say anything because what do you say to something like that? I waited. She said, "I do believe Ray loves that creature like his own child."

I stared at her.

"Truly," she said, nodding her head, as if confiding a deep secret, "or why would he keep Sokar at all? An untrainable animal is a dead animal, as far as they are concerned. They wanted to sell him to a big city zoo, and Ray paid for him instead, brought him home."

There were other pictures in her album. In one was a cage with several cubs of different kinds of cats—I couldn't recognize them, but they looked like tiger, black panther, clouded leopard. People were in the cages with them, feeding them milk with bottles. Children, too. I pointed. "What's that?"

"Oh, that's a petting zoo the breeding facility runs. They make the money for the adults that way. People love to see the cubs. That was a hit. We let people pet Sokar, too, in the early days, when he was small. See?"

She lifted up an old color photograph of a little spotted

cub running free in a fenced backyard with a deck and trees, children running behind him. "He loved to play ball," she said, pointing to a bright blue-and-white striped beach ball rolling ahead of the cub.

I was astonished. "He was out of the cage then?"

"Oh, yes," said Janet. "Why, he slept on our bed at night. He was just the happiest leopard cub you ever saw." She looked regretful. "We lived in a big neighborhood then. Lots of kids, families. Kids would come to play with Sokar. We took him trick-or-treating—everyone got a big kick out of it. Look at this one!"

I looked. Sokar was on a chair, paws on the dining table. Someone was holding a cookie toward him, and he was leaning forward to get it, his small cub face thin and eager, in his eyes a look I found strangely appealing: of playful, questioning curiosity.

"Little Sokar," she said with fondness. She smoothed the photo down with her fingers. "I loved little Sokar. He was like a child to me."

She blew her nose, hobbled over to the sink, washed her hands. I stole a look—her cheeks were damp.

I surveyed the photos scattered on the table. The cub photos all showed him free, or on a leash walking with Ray, eating out of a bowl in the kitchen, sitting with them on the couch.

"What happened?" I said at last. "Why did you cage him?"

"Oh, he got big," she said. "He got big, and he got crazy. He started to lash out at us when he couldn't get his own way. We fed him raw chicken and turkey meat, raw pork loin or steak. He wouldn't let us put the food down anymore. Then his play got rough, too. He ripped up Ray's arm more than once, and he bit me on the knee when I wouldn't play with him. We had to put him in a cage." She shook her head. "He didn't like it one bit, I can tell you that. He threw himself on the bars. Snarled and growled and hated on us."

I heard a low growling sound at just that moment. I was standing half in the dining room and half in the living area, and I looked across and saw Sokar. He was standing facing me, eyes unflinching. I felt a shiver go down my spine. I tried to reconcile him with the pictures of the playful cub I had seen.

At some point Janet told me the name *Sokar* came from Egypt; it meant god of the underworld. "It suits him, don't you think?"

Oh yes, I thought, *oh my, yes*. Those eyes had looked through and beyond me, as if he saw a world around us we couldn't see ourselves.

. . .

Once he knew freedom, of a kind.

So long ago the memory comes to him in a brassy haze, hot rush of pleasure, gold sun on limbs, muscles lithe and flexed (he was running), limbs freed and limbs stretching, he turns toward the bars in the back, the sides, the sight of the selfsame flaccid body wrapped around itself, he dismisses it as a dream, a longing.

He dreamed often of running.

He dreamed of the dark, and running.

Once he saw a trail, a stream, a pouring of water on rocks. Dark lapping on stones, tendrils and reaches of ice-cold water making a path through night. Owl call, sleep-rustle of wings, night things, sloth in trees, tiny mice, fashioned hands, digging a way through night. It was a dream.

He walked with another in the dark, walked through stripe and scar of moonlight, listened. They pounced, she and he. No mouse escaped them. Eyes froze, voices strummed out a call for release—they pounced, claw on pulse, teeth on throat. They fed in darkness. Moon cold on shoulders, night wind blowing.

In words before words, ways before ways are taught to him, the cold unforgettable knowing swims easy through limbs: how to watch, to wait; how to stalk, to kill.

...

Then we all had that one experience you never want to have, a pounding on the door at three in the morning, darkness sitting in the fields like a stone, and an officer of the law on the doorstep, grim about the mouth, saying, "Exotic animal alert." And we blinked in our dressing gowns, fresh from our dreams, unsure if we were trapped in a nightmare we could not remove ourselves from, cold from the screeching wind that blew in through the door.

"There's a leopard on the loose," he was saying next, and we screamed or gasped and clutched our throats, peering over his shoulder at his squad car, blue lights spinning in the driveway. "Where," we implored, "where?"

"No one knows," he was saying. "We're going from house to house now. He's already mauled one person, the owner's wife—she's been airlifted to a hospital in Chicago."

And it *was* a nightmare. We slammed into our houses when he left; we peered through windows at the shrubbery; we turned the television on and stared, white-faced, at the screen, the news very sparse just then. We knew as the Lord made daylight that this day was coming; we had warned about just such a thing. But no, the city let him put up that zoo of his and bring a grown leopard into a residential community—the county, the state, the whole benighted country let him. No one took our safety into consideration. A pet leopard—if such a thing can exist. And what had he done? He had escaped, as wild animals will. Except this wasn't the wild; it was a slow rural place, maybe, but we had no rainforest. We had open fields, open lots, cattails in swamps, and young trees. Some deer to kill, raccoons, fox, rabbits—and plenty of humans.

We thought of Janet Mertens, sitting next to his cage, being mauled to pieces. *Who would be next?* we wondered.

...

I had feared for Janet's life even as I sat beside her, beside a full-grown leopard. There was something so unnaturally still about him, it was sinister. I have heard of animals being slavishly devoted to their owners; I have heard of people being in love with their animals. But I saw none of that here. This leopard was watchful, wary. He was long past that time of cubhood, when they'd given him the taste of freedom, and whatever the past held—all those photos of freedom and fun—now the Mertens seemed to have a peculiar, antagonistic relationship with him, Ray especially.

I saw this in action myself, and I was afraid to tell anyone what I had seen. That is why I didn't, not until the whole thing unraveled before us.

Just before I left that day, Ray Mertens came into the room, and the first thing I saw was that his eyes were on the leopard. It was as if they locked gazes and neither would back down. The leopard growled. I felt bile rise high. I grabbed my purse. Ray took a stick and headed toward the cage. I wanted to run out the door, but he was between me and the door. He advanced with the stick, and the leopard was snarling now, a deep, angry sound. The two of us ladies—we were frozen on the couch.

Ray took another slow, meaningful step.

Janet quavered, "Why, Ray, what is it this time?"

And Ray said, not looking, still stealthily advancing, "Just showing him."

He plunged the stick in through the bars, and the leopard leapt back, snarling, and then the stick waved through the air, and although he was crouched as far back as he could go, it hit him, glancing sideways off the side of his head, and he snarled and whimpered and went down on his knees.

I got up then and went straight to the door. Behind me Janet was saying, in a thread-like voice, "Stop, Ray, please stop! You're hurting him."

"You stay out of this."

At the door I turned and saw the look on Janet's face as she gazed up at her once circus-trainer husband. She was open-mouthed, as if she had never encountered this darkness before in him. Her hands twisted each other in her lap. She had forgotten my presence. She was terrified, but not of the leopard.

I saw Ray's muscles taut in his back. The stick was flying in and out, rattling the bars. Sokar growled and dodged its continuous thrusts.

I was brought up never to tell someone to his face what I thought he should or should not do. I felt an urge to cry out, but I was afraid for my life. I was a coward; I could not speak; I could not tell this man he should not do this to a caged animal.

From the door I called, loudly, "I'll see you later, Janet!" I almost ran to my car in the driveway. There was something wrong with the Mertens, I thought, something terribly wrong with them.

· · ·

Because the man never opened the cage anymore.
Because the woman had slid back the latch with her own

hands, offering him the cold dead body of a hen, all memory of
running in her stilled. Dead unmoving hen.

Because, in leaping forward, the door swung open, and she
was in the way, and his body, entered upon the secret dream of
running, in the narcotic grip of forward motion, lunged at her,
claws out, teeth bared, not wanting her body in itself—it was in
the way—and he leapt on her.

. . .

They posted flyers around for miles, and they combed
the area, day in, day out, with helicopters and searchlights
and armed men searching the hills, but they didn't find that
leopard. The flyer comprised a grainy color photograph with
those yellow eyes and darkly spotted skin, the words *Exotic*
Animal Alert: Please Post Widely, a reward of $1,000, and a
phone number. Ray Mertens tended the zoo, and the media
dug up all the stories they could about the animal. We saw
pictures of the leopard as a cub, so loving and affectionate,
sleeping at the foot of their bed. And then he grew bigger, and
there was a video of him leaping up at a visitor at the petting
zoo, a young man who leapt back, and the leopard leapt again,
as if playful, and the boy fell and hurt his head on a rock;
the leopard leapt on him where he lay, and then Ray Mertens
jumped into the cage with his stick and scared him away. We
saw photos of the cage covered with tarpaulin so the leopard
couldn't look out, and one of his face bleeding where he had
hit it against the bars, repeatedly, trying to escape. We saw
how this leopard's life had changed from when he was a cub
to now, those bars before his bleeding face.

Then came the sightings, one after another. Sue Tisdale
saw a dark shape slink along behind her blackberry bushes
one evening, and she screamed and almost fainted. By the

time the police came, there was nothing there. Della and Rick Bourne were driving home from church one foggy morning when Sokar crossed the road in the fog, right in front of them, as they turned into their lane. He looked neither left nor right, they said; he just crossed, and the woods and fog swallowed him. The cops could not find him then, either. The woods went over hills and streams and open fields and acres of swamp. There were several hundred acres of woods there, between Gretchen and Dunston, close to the river. But this leopard didn't go into those woods and disappear. People thought he was skulking right about where the Mertens lived, that he hadn't left the area. And then, so many people saw movement in the shrubbery, light glancing off an amber eye, a muscled shoulder; or they heard a growl, a sudden snarl. The county was spooked. It was a terrible summer. The alerts were read out on the news, night after night.

Ray Mertens even showed up in the news; he said he had seen the cat a few times, skulking about near the tiger cages. He sounded jaunty and cocksure on television, said he was gonna get that animal himself. He had a gun in his hands, and he was climbing the hill behind his zoo, entering the woods as he spoke to the cameraman. He knew what that leopard was going to do—he was going to come back—and Ray cocked the rifle and aimed it at the dark trees, and when he came, Ray said, he was going to be ready for him.

. . .

Night, with the tigers asleep and the panthers awake and the monkeys up on their perch in their cages. Night sounds. Rustlings in the leaves: mice, voles. A screech owl tearing through the darkness. Low stir of wings.

In these woods are deer, and the first night he catches a fawn, tears it apart with his teeth, leaving the hollowed shell of ribs and pelvic bones in his lair.

Night after night he stalks creatures unused to being stalked. Two rabbits, a squirrel, a muskrat, down by the stream.

He sleeps in a drainage tunnel, deep in the center of it, with the bones around him, and dead leaves, and spiders spinning silver webs across the entrance.

But he cannot leave this place. Night after night he is drawn to the house. One night, he makes it all the way up to the door. Up on the grass, up against the window. There he sees him, the man of sticks, rifle across his knees, looking up at the window. There is no time to think. He leaps upward at the glass in a ferocity of snarling. The man swings, races for the door, and he backs into shrubs. The man comes out shooting. The sound of the gun going off makes him tremble and cower and rage. He pushes deeper into the shrubs. When the door opens, he springs.

...

I looked up Sokar, the ancient Egyptian god of the underworld, when I got home that day. For no reason, really. Just curiosity. He was a god who was depicted in various forms, often a falcon, for his divine ability to fly through the underworld, the earthworld, the heavens. Sometimes he was a falcon head, mounted in a book. Sometimes he was a mummified human form and sometimes a mummified falcon form. He often wore the conical crown with disc heads and cobras, similar to the atef crown of Osiris, god of fertility, god of death, god of life on earth, with whom he is often equated. He is known also as the god of rebirth and transfiguration. I looked at one picture of the mummified human form for a long time. He is upright, and his whole body is shrouded. Images of falcons are inscribed on the black shroud. His face is hidden, and only eyes look out—painted, stylized eyes.

. . .

When the shots sounded that night, we learned the Collinses called the police to come investigate. They knocked on the door, but no one answered. Janet was still in the hospital. The police broke down the front door, searched the house. There was no sign of Ray Mertens. Then they found him, just out of the family room, his body half in the room, sprawled against the cage, his arms and chest outside on the steps, his rifle a few steps away. His upper body was twisted and mangled, his face torn to pieces. The leopard had got his throat, and parts of his neck hung down in strips.

The leopard was not in sight. The noise of the police's arrival must have scared him off. But one officer stepping out into the grass to inspect the damaged peonies saw him. He had not gone away. He was in the bushes, waiting. The way we heard it, the officer pointed his rifle at the creature, and in that moment he sprang at them. He sprang at them, snarling, and the guns went off. He mauled one officer and leapt at another, and when they finally got him, they had downed one officer with their own bullets. But they got the cat twice, in the heart and the head. They called for backup and for an ambulance for the officer and the cold body of Ray Mertens, and the news was all over town the next day.

That's how the leopard was killed, and, later on, the state gave the animals to sanctuaries and closed the zoo, and Janet moved away to live with a niece in Indiana. We put it behind us; we moved on. It was only when one of us drove out near the swamp or on dark winter nights when a hunter saw a sudden shape near the stream that we remembered.

The night it all happened, no one had thought to protect Janet in the hospital. She learned about him there in the hospital, from the nightly news, when the graphic pictures of the yellow, spotted cat lying in a bed of crushed rose-colored peonies flashed on the screen. The nurses said she stared and whispered, "Little Sokar!" She must have thought of the past; images of his life must have flashed before her eyes. In one stroke, too, she had lost her husband, and she went hysterical, weeping. But I thought it was not for her husband; she had only feared him. "My baby, my baby," she cried, and wept.

Vivarium

Claire Ibarra

STAND ON LEFT FOOT, then right foot, back to left foot, switch to right foot, snap fingers five times, blink five times, count by fives to fifty and count down.

That was Eva's ritual whenever she felt anxious, which was many times throughout the course of a day. Anything—gusty winds, shrill noises, spoiled food in the refrigerator, a conversation with a stranger—was enough to set her off. Now it was the monstrous, hideous cockroach that had just dashed across the room and now hid under the kitchenette cabinet.

Eva was still adjusting to her studio apartment in Miami Beach, after leaving her parents and childhood home in Connecticut. She was twenty-three and working on her master's degree in clinical counseling. This was the first time she'd lived alone.

She would look out the window at the suntanned girls rollerblading in bikini tops and shorts, swaying their hips from side to side as guys rubbernecked. Convertibles cruised by blasting rap, and tourists wearing flamboyant colors strolled along the sidewalk. Before closing the blinds and returning to her studies, Eva considered how she ended up here: It was her father who decided that Miami Beach would force Eva out of her shell.

Now she curled up on the lumpy cushioned armchair and watched the crack under the cabinet. Her eyes never left the black, tiny crevice on the linoleum floor. Five, ten, fifteen, twenty … Eva waited and watched. Fifteen minutes passed.

Her laptop was within reach, so she Googled *cockroach*. She discovered on Wikipedia that thirty cockroach species out of forty-five hundred are associated with human habitats, and that four species are considered pests. The article went on to say that cockroaches live in a wide range of environments, prefer warm conditions found within buildings, and exhibit complex behaviors associated with group-based decision-making.

When Eva looked up, she let the laptop fall to her side and hugged her legs into her chest. The monster had crawled out of the crack and was scuttling toward her. Eva crinkled her face into a tight ball. Snap five times, blink five times, and count by fives to fifty.

The cockroach stopped a few feet away. Eva shut her eyes tight. She held her breath for as long as she could. After several minutes, she opened one eye, then the other. She and the cockroach were at a standstill. Since it was frozen in its path, Eva took a moment to observe. It was the biggest bug she had ever seen—bigger than a dragonfly, bigger than a grasshopper. It had a flat, broad body with a glossy exoskeleton, an armor a nasty color of brown tinged with green and yellow. The color reminded her of the time she got food poisoning from tainted Mexican food.

Eva realized that most people would just squish a bug. But how does one squish a colossal-size bug and cope with real guts, not just a black smudge to be flicked away with a fingernail? Getting rid of this cockroach would be like scooping up roadkill.

The cockroach waved its long antennae and made a quick spurt closer. Eva screamed and tucked her legs into her chest tighter. She took the throw pillow from behind her back and tossed it on the cockroach. The pink satin pillow landed right on top of it. Eva let out a deep breath and moaned.

Eva cautiously tiptoed across the small room and grabbed her phone. She sat on the futon cross-legged so that her feet were off the floor. She had the apartment manager's phone number under favorites, just like her dad had told her to do.

"Hello, Señora Gonzalez. This is Eva in apartment 5A. I need you to come right away. I have an emergency," Eva yelled into her cell.

"What kind of emergency, *niña*?" the manager yelled back.

Eva held the phone away from her ear and answered, "There's a cockroach in my apartment. I need you to come catch it."

"Ay, *mi hija*. I don't have time for that right now. We have a leak from upstairs. There's a plumber waiting for me outside. You'll have to do it yourself."

"But how?" Eva pleaded. She felt panic set in again. Blink five times.

"*Escucha*. You just grab it with a paper towel and flush it down the toilet. Or you can get a broom, smash it, and sweep it up. It's not a big deal."

"I can't do it," Eva whined.

"*Bueno*, it's your fault. Maybe next time you'll let the exterminator into your apartment," the manager told her and then abruptly hung up. Eva could imagine the thoughts going through Señora Gonzalez's mind: spoiled *gringa*, little princess, Daddy's girl.

Eva did regret not letting the exterminator into her apartment two weeks ago. He had appeared at her door wearing a uniform and dirty black boots. He pulled a small metal tank with a hose attached and tried to coax Eva into letting him in. "This is a building requirement; all of the units get sprayed," he had explained. But Eva couldn't stand the thought of poison contaminating her living area, where she slept and prepared food. And his boots were grimy and would have soiled the carpet. After she refused and he left, Señora Gonzalez called her on the phone, furious and warning that the next time she would have to let him in—pest control was part of maintenance and written into her lease agreement.

Eva felt tears spring up, and her chest tightened. She let out a sob. She looked over at the pillow, and nothing appeared to move. She half-expected the pillow to roll over, as if the titan cockroach could lift or scoot it out of its way. She decided to call her mother.

"Hello?" her mother answered.

"Mom, I'm so glad you answered. I have an emergency, and I don't know what to do," Eva cried into the phone.

"Eva, is that you? What's happened? Do we need to call the police? Tell me you're okay, please." Eva's mother was hypersensitive by nature—or possibly by nurture, from her twenty-six-year marriage to a domineering husband.

Eva couldn't answer right away as she tried to stop the sobs.

Her mother continued, "Listen, Eva. If you're in danger, I want you to hang up and dial 911, right now, do you understand me?"

"No, Mom. I'm okay. I'm sorry I scared you, but there's a huge cockroach in my apartment. It's trapped under a pillow right now, but I don't know how to kill it. I know it sounds silly, but it's huge and ugly, and I'm afraid to touch it." Eva suddenly felt childish. She was angry with herself for being so weak and inept, just the way her father believed she was, the way he insinuated with underhanded comments, always muttered under his breath, *Let me do it, this is a man's job, girls will be girls ...*

Eva's mom asked, "A cockroach? Have you been keeping your place clean?"

Eva was surprised by the question, as if there could be any doubt. She scrubbed and cleaned on a regular basis, as she couldn't sleep at night with the thought of a dirty dish in the sink or even a picture hanging crooked on the wall. Eva glanced over at the spray bottle of Formula 409 with bleach on the counter.

"Very clean, Mom. Señora Gonzalez says that this is their natural habitat because of the humidity and warm weather. It's not like up north, where they infest garbage. The cockroaches in Florida even fly, and they're as big as bats." Eva felt herself on the verge of a hysterical rant.

"I'm sorry I can't help you, sweetie. Maybe you could ask Señora Gonzalez, or a neighbor, or—oh, wait, what do you say? Here, honey—"

Suddenly her dad was on the line. "Eva, what's this about a roach? Are you kidding me?"

"Dad, I really don't like it here."

"Listen, it's all for the best. Right now, you need to suck it up and calm down. It's only a bug, so squash it. Women. You can't expect a man to always be there to do your dirty work. I'm passing you back to your mother."

Her mother said in a gentle, soft voice, "Call me back when it's over, so I know you're okay."

Eva crept over to the armchair, where she had a better view of the pillow. Snap five times, blink five times, count by fives to fifty and count down. She stretched out her leg and, with her toes, Eva ever so slowly and cautiously lifted the pillow an inch, two inches, three inches, then all the way over. There was nothing. No cockroach. Eva quickly snatched her leg back up to her chest. She looked around the room.

The hideous beast rested in a corner, right next to the bathroom. It was still except for the thin, long antennae, which moved through the air as if searching for a signal. Eva thought about her neighbors. There was another girl who lived next door. They had spoken a couple of times, but Eva knew they could never be friends. Victoria had a boyfriend who was always around, and lots of people who stopped by, and there were parties, music, and the smell of pot. Eva felt too mousy to hang out with a girl like that. Eva had never seen the other neighbor; she wasn't even sure someone lived there. There were other people in the building, mostly young, hipster types, and one outrageously cute guy. She would die before she talked to him.

Eva contemplated going to Victoria's apartment to ask for help, but she felt embarrassed. She was stuck with the cockroach; they were bound together by fate. Eva sat curled up on the armchair and watched the cockroach; it, too, seemed transfixed, perhaps by watching her. She listened to the tick of the clock hanging on the wall. Her eyelids began to feel heavy, and she relaxed her head back on the soft cushion.

It was almost dark outside. The room was dim, and she could hear the deep bass of music playing next door and shouting in the street. She looked over, and the cockroach was still in the same spot.

Eva began to think about her resources, tools she had inside her apartment that could be used for capturing, if not killing, the bug. In the kitchenette was a broom and dustpan—probably her best bet for getting the job done. There were also Tupperware containers and plastic grocery bags. Any of these items could be used to dispose of the monstrous creature. It was just so massive, and repulsive, and most likely quick when the chase was on.

Eva ran into the kitchen, grabbed the broom and dustpan from the pantry closet, and jumped back onto the armchair. She held the broom out like a sword. The cockroach was eerily still, except the antennae, always waving and searching. As

Eva prepared her attack, she began to realize the logistical difficulties of the long broom handle and the small, short-handled dustpan. She couldn't see a way to avoid getting her hand perilously close to the creature. Grasping onto the dustpan meant putting her fingers in harm's way. Snap five times. Blink five times. Eva was exhausted.

She suddenly ran back into the kitchen and grabbed a large plastic Tupperware container, round and wide. Without overthinking, Eva approached the cockroach, hoping to catch it by surprise, and quickly placed the container over the bug. Afraid of the cockroach's perceived mighty strength, she tapped the side of the makeshift bell jar to test its durability. She felt triumphant.

Eva knelt and cautiously crawled around the specimen, observing it through the transparent plastic. It slowly moved itself to the rim, and Eva didn't flinch, even though she could see its legs go up and down, as if it were doing push-ups, and its long feelers scanned the air, as if surveying Eva's aura. Now that it was trapped, Eva discovered that she could observe the bug at her leisure, without fear.

She sat and watched, listening to shrieks of laughter and Coldplay blasting from Victoria's apartment, while something she had read on Wikipedia nagged at her—the fact that cockroaches exhibited complex behaviors associated with group-based decisions. She began to think that perhaps she and the bug had solidarity in their loneliness. They were both social creatures, stuck alone, longing to connect to others of their species. Count by fives to fifty and count down. Eva crawled over to the futon and fell asleep.

The next morning, Eva checked briefly on the cockroach before getting ready for the day. It lay motionless, so she showered, dressed, and poured a bowl of Cheerios. While eating, she thought again about the cockroach living in her homemade vivarium and what it would need to survive.

How much water? What does it eat? She thought most likely anything. Eva Googled and learned that cockroaches could survive days, up to a week, without water. And indeed they would eat anything—even hair and books—any sort of decaying matter. Eva shuddered at the thought, then blinked five times and snapped five.

It was Saturday, so Eva spread out her assignments and books to study, making herself comfortable on the futon. She could observe the cockroach from there while reading *The Adolescent in Family Therapy, Second Edition*. Being at the center of a dysfunctional nuclear family had inspired Eva to become a family therapist. She figured she could relate to kids with OCD and depression, help them learn to manage and cope, even if they were never completely cured. Eva knew these were lifelong battles.

A couple of hours passed, and Eva took a break to make a sandwich and check on the cockroach. To her surprise, the cockroach was lying on its back, with its long legs wiggling frantically in all directions. It had most likely tried to climb up the side of the slippery container and had fallen backwards. Once on its back, a cockroach cannot flip itself over, Eva learned by observing the creature—a surprising defect for one of the most ancient evolutionary species, for a species thought to be able to out-survive all the others after a global disaster.

Its abdomen was grotesque and frightening, like an alien creature. Its six long, hairy legs protruded out from a segmented stomach, and they jerked through the air desperately. Eva was mortified by its ugliness at first, but gradually she got used to the underside of her beastly companion. Then she felt sorry for it in its helpless state. She thought for a while about how she could aid the bug without actually touching it. Eva remembered that she had ordered Chinese food a few days ago.

Eva opened the drawer in the kitchen and pulled out a set of chopsticks. She broke apart the two wood sticks and took one over to the cage. Tucking the stick inside from the bottom, she gently flipped the cockroach over. Eva then felt compelled to do more, so she took a small piece of foil and molded a tiny dish, filling it with tap water, then got a piece of bread crust. She quickly lifted one side of the vivarium and placed the water and bread inside. With her mission complete, Eva blinked five times, snapped five times, and began to count.

While eating a peanut butter and jelly sandwich, Eva read more on the Internet. She learned that cockroaches have a brain, heart, colon, reproductive system, and that their eyes have more than a thousand lenses, allowing them to see from multiple angles at once.

A knock at the door jerked Eva to attention. "Who's there?" she called from across the room. The only answer was another bang on the door.

When Eva looked through the peephole, she saw Victoria, holding a pitcher.

"Dude, my water was cut by the imbecile plumber. Do you have water?" Victoria asked with irritation, while holding the empty pitcher out to Eva.

"Oh, yeah, hi. I do." Eva took the pitcher and gestured for Victoria to come in. Eva had forgotten about her pet cockroach. At first, Victoria didn't notice as they stood together at the kitchen sink while Eva filled the pitcher. There was an awkward silence, until Eva asked, "How's school?"

"I dropped out. My mom got laid off, so I had to get a job. Now I'm waitressing full-time," Victoria said casually.

Eva admired Victoria's tough, cool attitude. She liked Victoria's jet-black hair with its one streak of hot pink, her eyebrow piercing, and the heart tattoos on her wrists. Eva said, "Well, there's always next semester." She felt like a major dork.

But then Victoria's attention was drawn to the plastic Tupperware on the carpet.

"What's that over there?" Victoria began to approach with curiosity.

"It's nothing," Eva replied nervously, trailing behind Victoria.

Victoria bent and peered down into the container, getting the full 360-degree view. "Oh my God. What the hell is that?"

Eva tried to imagine how it would look to someone else, the tiny foil dish of water, the crust of bread, and the disgusting cockroach in her homemade insectarium. She began a rant: "There was this cockroach loose in my apartment, and I didn't know how to catch it, and the pillow didn't work, and the dustpan has a short handle—not a long, standing one like my mom's—and then it fell onto its back and couldn't roll back over, and it can survive one week without water, but I learned that cockroach fossils date back two hundred and eighty million years, and they have a heart and brain, and they make group-based decisions, which means they are social, like humans, but this one is alone, like me—" Eva paused for a breath.

"Okay, hold on." Victoria knelt and peered more intently into the cage. "Relax for a minute. Look, it's eating the bread." Victoria pointed at the bug.

Eva knelt next to Victoria, and both watched intently as the cockroach sat on the piece of crust, moving its head from side to side. Just then, Eva thought about her father and his probable outrage at her handling of the bug. She could imagine his accusations: tree hugger, socialist, vegetarian— like those degenerate, flaky hippies.

"Does it have a name?" Victoria asked.

"Chico." The name just popped out.

Victoria said, "Chico *la Cucaracha*, that's fucking awesome. I didn't know you had it in you, Eva. You got your freak flag flying!"

Eva smiled at the thought of a freak flag. She was always more concerned with doing everything right, having everything perfect, than with having any fun, or even being happy. "Yeah, I guess I do."

"Hey, can my boyfriend come over to see this?"

"Sure."

"We'll come over around eight, and then we're headed to a party in North Beach. You wanna come with us? It'll be cool, I promise." Victoria had softened her voice. She looked Eva in the eyes, like a much wiser, kinder version of Victoria. "Do you want to take Chico with us?" she asked.

"No, he'll be better off here."

Yet Eva was worried, and she felt a pang of guilt. Cockroaches live in groups and make decisions collectively. Eva realized that he was a social creature and shouldn't be left alone.

Julia and the Sea Bear

Nels Hanson

PERHAPS IF YOU LIVE IN CALIFORNIA and have traveled to the sea, or have visited the state and its beautiful coastline, you stopped along Highway 1, and from the cliffs beside the road you saw a strange creature walking alone along the distant beach.

That stretch of coast and the Sea Bear's beach lie between two cities, San Luis Obispo to the south and Monterey to the north. If you were very lucky, you might have stopped outside the little town called Blue Cove and seen the Sea Bear.

That's where he lived for five years, until one early morning a few months ago, when he disappeared and everyone wondered where he had gone.

The Sea Bear was famous, and tourists used to stop their cars in the special turnout by the cliffs above his beach. The coastal park rangers had installed several telescopes you could look through for fifty cents. You could watch the brown, full-grown Sea Bear sleep outside his cave in the warm sand or walk on all fours along the surf line with his nose to the moist, dark sand at low tide.

On foggy, disappointing days, he still might appear—suddenly, out of nowhere, like a dream creature emerging from an ancient mist.

At morning and evening, the Sea Bear approached the breaking waves on two legs and waded out into the ocean for his breakfast and dinner. With his right paw, he caught silver, black-striped perch and other small fish that came close to land. He saw them shining in the surf as they darted through the salt water the Sea Bear never drank. He drank only from a pure stream that made a little pool in the far back corner of his stone cave.

In the early days of the Sea Bear's appearance, there wasn't a fence along the cliff, and people could walk right up to the edge and drop things to the Sea Bear. Sometimes parents and children dropped sandwiches or bags of potato chips or apples and oranges for the Sea Bear to eat. The cliffs were almost three hundred feet high, and the snacks that friendly tourists tossed to the Sea Bear were smashed and covered with fine sand after they landed.

Often children wrote notes to the Sea Bear, tied them to pebbles, and threw them over the cliff for the Sea Bear to read. One day a boy and a girl each dropped a message to the Sea Bear with a blank page attached and a little pencil taped to the paper for the Sea Bear to write them back.

But the Sea Bear couldn't read or write. He walked from his cave and sniffed the letters and pencils. He looked up at the high cliffs and saw the boy and the girl waving, and then without raising a paw he turned and walked toward the sea for his early evening meal.

The boy was especially disappointed, but his mother asked him to think how the Sea Bear could have returned the boy's note to the high cliff.

"Maybe he could find an old bottle washed up on shore and put his letter into the bottle and find a cork to keep the water out," the boy answered. "He could throw the bottle into the sea, and maybe later someone might find it on some beach and send it to me."

"I don't think it would matter," the boy's mother answered. "The Sea Bear can't speak or write human words to answer his friends, even if he could take the letter to the post office."

"How do you know the Sea Bear can't talk or write to humans?" the boy answered. "Have you talked to him or asked him to read to you from a book? No one has because we're up here, and the Sea Bear is way down there."

That was before the rangers put up the high fence and the signs warning tourists not to throw food or paper or blankets down to the Sea Bear.

The rangers were worried the Sea Bear might get sick from eating unfamiliar food. The Sea Bear already had several beach blankets and striped towels that people had seen him drag into his cave to make a bed. He didn't need any more warm covers, and the rangers didn't want the Sea Bear's beach to become littered.

The Sea Bear's private beach was surrounded on three sides by the cliffs that were almost impossible to climb. Only a champion mountaineer might have climbed down the tall walls of rock. Yellow signs warned climbers not to try to descend the cliffs and bother the Sea Bear, who could only run into his cave or swim out into the ocean to escape intruders. The fine for trespassing on the Sea Bear's home ground was $10,000.

The only access to the Sea Bear's beach was by the ocean, but it was against the law to land a boat on the beach or to approach any closer than 500 yards. Sometimes motorboats and sailboats zigzagged back and forth, trying to catch a glimpse of the Sea Bear. Each day the rangers' bright white boat, flying the California state flag with its brown grizzly bear, patrolled the waters and protected the Sea Bear's shore. If airplanes or helicopters flew lower than 2,000 feet above the Sea Bear's portion of coastline, the rangers turned in the law-breaking pilots to the Civil Air Patrol.

Once a diver in a black rubber suit and goggles surfaced in a wave, and in his flippers he began walking toward the dry sand. Tourists on the cliff saw the Sea Bear run from his cave and hurry toward the diver, who quickly turned and dived back into the surf.

Did the Sea Bear think the man in his dark suit and mask was another bear and ran to meet him?

Was the Sea Bear hungry and thought the man might be good to eat, a nice switch from the silvery fish he always ate?

No one was sure. An amateur birdwatcher shot a video of the Sea Bear and the frightened human diver, and it played on the TV news. Worried fans of the Sea Bear called the station and then wrote letters to the newspaper, filling a whole page with the same message: *Leave our Sea Bear alone!*

The sudden trespassing on the Sea Bear's beach gained a lot of attention, and the newspaper ran old stories of the Sea Bear's first appearance and his life on the beach by the gray sandstone cliffs. The stories quoted the opinions of scientists who were experts on bears, and of marine biologists who knew all about the animals who lived in and beside the sea.

Still, five years after the Sea Bear had first been seen on the isolated beach, no one had learned where he had come from or how, and almost no one agreed about the Sea Bear's original home.

One boy who wrote a letter to the paper thought the Sea Bear had been captured up in Canada for a zoo. As the zoo ship passed with many animals in their cages, the Sea Bear, who was very strong, bent open the bars of his jail and dived into the ocean and swam to the beach, vowing that he would never be recaptured alive.

A teacher at the elementary school suggested that the Sea Bear and his mother had wandered down from the Coast Range Mountains during a drought year to fish in the sea. The young bear had run ahead of his mother and fallen from the cliff. Luckily, the cub landed on a big soft pile of wet seaweed left by a recent storm and survived. His mother couldn't reach him but at least she knew he was all right. Finally, as night came on, she had re-crossed the busy road and climbed back into the mountains without her cub, who from then on was the Sea Bear.

A local palm reader who wore a swami's blue satin turban with a big red rhinestone at the front insisted the Sea Bear had once been a man, a pioneer who had been a cruel hunter. After he died and spent more than a hundred years as windblown dust, the hunter had been reborn as the lonely Sea Bear to learn his lesson, "to walk in someone else's paws," as Madame Zorra explained.

An old man who had been a sailor and fisherman claimed he knew how the Sea Bear had arrived on the beach. As a young man on a fishing trawler off the coast of Oregon, he had seen a brown bear cub clinging to a floating log that had washed down a raging river from the forest. The fisherman wanted to rescue the cub, but the captain said he didn't want any animals on his boat except for flopping fish. The little bear cried helplessly as the current took his log farther out to sea, but all the worried fisherman could do was throw the cub a red salmon, which he caught in his paws. The old fisherman always felt guilty about not saving the baby bear. He said that the Sea Bear was the cub who had survived when his one-log raft washed up near Blue Cove.

A husband and wife who made a good living selling Sea Bear items from their gift shop just north of the cliffs had their own idea. They said the Sea Bear only appeared now and then, like Tinker Bell in Peter Pan. If good children wished for him before they went to sleep, they would see him the next day when they went with their parents to the cliffs above his beach. That's how the Sea Bear had first arrived. Children's wishes had brought him to Blue Cove.

No one—not fortune-tellers or scientists or rangers or old fishermen or gift-shop owners or anyone else—could prove where the Sea Bear came from. Most who read the newspaper or watched the news on TV decided that the story of the Sea Bear's earliest years would always remain a mystery.

The important thing was that the Sea Bear lived undisturbed on his beach. When they saw him from the cliffs, or saw a picture a photographer had taken with a telescopic lens, local residents felt a strong affection for their Sea Bear and wondered what his life alone on the beach was really like.

Was the Sea Bear happy?

Did he have enough to eat?

Did he get tired of eating fish?

If you dropped some blackberry seeds, could they grow in the sand and produce fruit the Sea Bear might like?

Did the Sea Bear get lonely for other bears?

Did the Sea Bear dream when he went to sleep?

If he did, what did he dream of?

Most people believed these questions would always remain without answers, until one day a strange thing happened. It was strange even for people who were used to living near the Sea Bear.

...

A girl who had just celebrated her ninth birthday passed through Blue Cove with her family. Like most other tourists, they had stopped on the cliff to see the Sea Bear, who was walking along the tideline by himself, his nose to the wet sand. Then they drove north on Highway 1 until they stopped at the Sea Bear gift shop and went inside.

The family looked at the toy Sea Bears and other things with the Sea Bear's name and picture: coffee cups, lunch boxes, backpacks, sweatshirts, and baseball caps. There were little glazed statuettes of the Sea Bear with two crystals for his eyes, and at the center of the shop stood a five-foot statue of the Sea Bear made of bronze.

Among the hundreds of Sea Bear items, only one caught the attention of the young girl, whose name was Julia. In a locked glass cabinet just below the wood counter, in a small, open blue box, was a tuft of brown fur. The sign inside the glass case read:

IS THIS THE SEA BEAR'S FUR?

The notice said that the fur had washed up a few miles down the coast and been identified by a college professor as bear fur. There hadn't been any bears sighted along the California coast for many years, and it was highly possible that the fur belonged to the Sea Bear.

The tuft of hair might have come loose and floated away when the Sea Bear was fishing in the surf or taking a salty bath. It might have happened in the early summer, when he was shedding his winter fur.

Julia's family was on vacation from Florida, and her mother and father walked about the large gift shop. Julia remained by the glass cabinet, staring at the little box that held the bit of brown fur. It was late in the afternoon, past time for them to continue their drive up the coast, and Julia's parents walked up to their daughter to ask her if she would like one of the smaller, inexpensive brown Sea Bears with a little ribbon around its neck. It would be a special, extra birthday gift.

That's when Julia stood on tiptoe and whispered in her mother's ear.

Then a smiling woman behind the counter stepped over to the glass case and asked Julia's mother if they needed help with something.

The mother frowned, then gestured for the woman who ran the gift shop to lean closer.

Julia's mother explained in a lowered voice that since her daughter had been a baby she had shown special powers.

After Julia had just learned to walk, she had gone into her mother's bedroom and opened her mother's jewelry case, then held up a gold ring with a ruby and lettering etched around the red stone. The little girl had held out one hand, spreading her fingers, as if her hand made a web. Then she had held both of her hands together and swung back her arms, then swung her joined hands in a long sweep to hit at the air. Then, with a cupped hand, she pretended to throw some invisible thing toward the window.

To make a long story short, Julia's mother explained to the manager that her own father, Julia's grandfather, had been a baseball player for the New York Yankees. They had won the World Series in 1947, and the ring was a prize each player had received for winning the championship.

The manager was surprised and confused. She had met thousands of customers visiting Blue Cove and the Sea Bear. Lots of tourists had interesting stories to tell. But she had never heard of a child who could know the past by holding an old ring.

The woman didn't know what to say, or what Julia's mother really wanted, so she listened to a few more tales of magical feats Julia had performed.

When she was three, Julia had found an expensive lost watch by holding the gold chain the watch had fallen from. A year later, in a field of high grass, Julia recovered a box of keepsakes stolen from a neighbor's house when a robin called and told her the hiding place. At school, Julia could solve her math problems by just touching the numbers. A blue number would appear on her worksheet, and Julia would trace it with her pencil. It would always be the right answer.

"That's amazing," said the manager. She looked closely at Julia, whose head barely reached the top of the glass cabinet, then at Julia's father, who only smiled and agreed the stories his wife told were true. Then she looked back at Julia's mother. "What is it your daughter wants?" she asked.

Julia's mother said, "Could my daughter touch the fur, just for a minute?"

"We never let customers touch the Sea Bear's fur," said the woman. "Let me talk to my husband."

The woman turned and went into a back room while Julia kept staring at the Sea Bear's fur, running her palm along the glass, as if to pet a part of the Sea Bear's brown coat, the same color as her own hair.

"It's highly unusual," said the woman's husband when he appeared. "We've never had a request like this before. No one has touched the Sea Bear's fur since the professor examined it under a microscope."

"I've gathered from reading that little booklet over there"—Julia's mother pointed to a wire book stand that held books with the Sea Bear's picture on the cover—"that no one knows the true story of the Sea Bear. Is that correct?"

"Yes," said the man, "no one knows."

"Well," said Julia's mother. "It might be worth a try. You never know about children and what special knowledge they have."

The man put his head next to his wife's, whispering in her ear, and his wife nodded. The man took out a silver ring that held many keys. He sorted through them until he found a large brass key that had tarnished because it was never used.

Carefully, he opened the cabinet. From behind the counter, he lifted the open blue box with the Sea Bear's fur and held it out, leaning toward Julia.

Julia looked up at her mother, then put out her hand, stroking the dry, rough fur. She let her hand go still, her fingertips resting on the fur, until she looked up at her mother and said, "That's enough. Now I know."

"What do you know, dear?" asked the man. "Can you tell me?"

"Yes," said Julia. "I saw it all very clearly."

Julia's mother put her hand on Julia's shoulder as Julia began to tell the Sea Bear's true story.

As Julia was talking, a young man who had entered the shop five minutes before took out a notebook and a pen. He had been listening to the conversation.

Julia spoke, and the young man wrote down her words carefully, then hurried outside to make a call on his cell phone. His name was Jerry, and he was a reporter for the Blue Cove newspaper. He had only been working for the paper for a week, but he was sure that he had just stumbled onto a scoop.

After Julia finished her story, she and her parents and the little stuffed Sea Bear they had bought for Julia's birthday continued their vacation and drove up the coast past Big Sur to Monterey.

Two days later, Julia's story appeared in the local paper. Suddenly, everyone in the town was talking again about the Sea Bear.

Julia's story was short and clear.

...

As a cub, the Sea Bear had lived in the forest high above Blue Cove. He had been in a meadow covered with yellow flowers that smelled sweet, with bees buzzing everywhere, when the Sea Bear's mother began looking toward the nearby oak trees where the bees might have their hive. She loved honey, and she was sure the young Sea Bear, who was just a regular cub and not the Sea Bear yet, would love honey, too. He had never tasted it because he was only six months old and had been born in the fall, during cold weather in the mountains. This was his first springtime, when the flowers were blooming and the bees were busy collecting sugary nectar.

The Sea Bear's mother walked over to the trees, looking left and right and lifting her muzzle to smell for honey. The Sea Bear, on his own, had followed a little green-and-yellow striped snake that was sliding through the grass toward a wall of rock that bordered the meadow. The snake disappeared, slipping down a hole at the base of some heavy rocks.

The young bear sniffed and searched for the little snake. He'd never seen one before and wanted to learn more about the sleek legless creature.

As he looked for the snake among the rocks, the ground shook under his paws. A big rock fell down a few feet away, scaring the Sea Bear, so he turned and ran back into the meadow. Then the ground quit shaking, and he looked back at the wall of rocks.

Something was different, and he noticed a door had opened among the rough broken stones. He walked up to it, sniffing as he went, and he put his head through the new opening in the rocks.

It was dusty in the dark hole, and his sneeze echoed and echoed, as if somewhere far below in the earth, another cub had sneezed.

The Sea Bear wanted to find the other bear hiding in the dark. Maybe the other bear was lost, or maybe he lived underground and they could meet and play together. Now the Sea Bear entered the hole, which was the entrance to a cave, and in the dark he moved farther and farther along a tunnel that kept growing more and more narrow.

Now and then he looked back at the small dot of sunlight

that shone at the opening of the passageway where he'd entered. Still, he kept going, in a hurry to meet the other cub. His breathing echoed off the walls of the tunnel, and he thought it was the quick breath of the other bear running toward him. The Sea Bear was frightened in the dark, and he started to run, to quickly find the other bear. Then the earth shook again.

As he ducked his head, big rocks fell down, and dust rose up.

When the earth was stable, he looked behind him; the path to the tunnel's opening in the meadow was blocked. He pawed at the fallen stones, but they were heavy and wouldn't budge. His only choice was to go farther along in the dark, to the other end of the tunnel, and that's what he did, for hours and hours until he felt like giving up.

Then he saw a light in the distance and heard something gurgling, then something watery crashing even louder. He ran toward the light and the two noises, and soon he came to a pool of water bubbling from a spring. His throat was dry from the dust of the falling rocks, and he leaned down to take several quick laps of cold, sweet water. Then he looked up. The tunnel had grown wider, and now he saw it was a cave with a wide door full of sunlight.

He crossed the smooth cave floor, and when he reached the opening, he ran out onto a sandy beach beside high cliffs, with the ocean in front of him.

The Sea Bear couldn't find the other cub, and he walked up and down the sand, past ocean waves that appeared to be alive. He walked up to them carefully and sniffed, then lapped with his tongue and spit out the salty water. He watched the seabirds fly above his head, for a moment wishing he were a seagull. The birds weren't lost. They knew where they were going.

As the sun began to turn orange and set into the ocean, the Sea Bear realized he was alone and lost. He looked back toward the entrance to the cave, but he knew it was no use to try to find his way back to the meadow. And so the Sea Bear slept that night in the cave, listening to the bubbling pool and to the waves.

The Sea Bear taught himself to fish, and he dragged the blankets tourists threw from the cliffs into his cave for a bed. He had no friends among the passing seagulls and the sea otters who paddled offshore on their backs. They always stared at him with uninterested eyes and went on toward their destinations.

His only acquaintance was a black harbor seal who sometimes appeared in the surf, barking for the Sea Bear. The Sea Bear would approach the waves and try to bark for a while before the seal turned and dived into the sea.

Maybe if the Sea Bear could've barked like the seal, the seal might have been less afraid and come closer. The only loud noise the Sea Bear could make was a howl, which sounded like twenty small growls put together.

Once, the Sea Bear saw that the seal had come up onto the land, and he ran forward to greet him. But then the creature turned and swam back out into the ocean. He saw the seal again a few days later, but the seal never swam so close to shore again. The Sea Bear never knew that the seal he had seen leaving the water wasn't really a seal, that it was a man in a black wetsuit who wanted to take his picture and sell it to a national magazine.

The Sea Bear didn't know that he had become famous, even when he sometimes saw the distant figures of the tourists at the top of the cliff, waving. He sensed they weren't bears and weren't like his friend the seal, and out of caution, he didn't wave back.

He never ate the food they dropped before the fence was put up along the cliff. He was afraid it was a trick to catch and hurt him. He never fished farther than fifty yards out into the sea, to stay far away from the boats that also held strange animals. They yelled and waved and lifted dark things to their eyes, as if aiming at him with short sticks.

The Sea Bear lived alone in his cave, napping by himself on the clean sand on warm days. For a long time he was lonely for his mother, and he would sometimes whimper a few times before he went to sleep. Then he became lonesome for other bears he had never met but that he had seen when he went for walks with his mother.

Years went by, and the Sea Bear slowly grew used to his loneliness.

He got up each morning and waded out to catch his breakfast. Then he walked along the beach sniffing the jellyfish and empty shells that had washed in during the night. He heard the seabirds' cries and watched their white wings passing. Sometimes he wished he could fly, past the cliffs and the blocked cave, and return to the forest to find his mother.

The Sea Bear's life kept to its unchanging, daily pattern, except during heavy storms and high waves, when the Sea Bear stayed in his dry cave. When the sun came out, he would hurry to the ocean to catch some silver fish to satisfy his hunger, running past the snarls of driftwood like old bones that had washed up.

Then one night the Sea Bear had a wonderful dream.

He dreamed that he was a bear but also a bird, a seagull, and he was crossing the ocean very fast, either flying or running easily along the tops of the waves, until up ahead he saw an island where he landed on his four paws.

He looked up with amazement at the brightly colored birds and the trees trailing long vines, at the leafy bushes with sweet, blue-and-orange fruit that he tasted and enjoyed. In the clearings he recognized some of the animals that his mother had pointed out to him when he was small: a fox, a deer, a wild pig, an opossum.

At the top of a tall green tree, he saw what looked like a squirrel except it didn't have a bushy tail but a long skinny tail that it used to swing from limb to limb.

As hard as he looked, exploring the strange island, he didn't see another bear. After a while he grew tired and, beside a meadow near a sheer, overgrown cliff, he lay down to sleep.

The Sea Bear dreamed that in the cliff wall there was an opening, a cave that led to a meadow, and in the meadow lived another bear, just one, who was lonely like himself. Each night when the other bear went to sleep, she dreamed of the lonely Sea Bear, his beach, and his cave.

The Sea Bear ran toward the brown bear in the meadow, and she ran toward him, but just as they got close enough to see each other's brown eyes, they both woke up. The pretty brown bear woke up on her island in the middle of the sea, and the Sea Bear woke in his cave on the beach.

Each night the Sea Bear dreamed of the bear on the island, and in his dream the bear on the island dreamed of him, but in the meadow where they almost met, they always woke before their noses could touch.

...

Julia and her parents had driven on to Monterey and then San Francisco, and then they drove all the way back to Florida. For a month, they didn't know that Julia's story had appeared in the paper, the story that everyone in Blue Cove read and was talking about. People wrote letters to the paper, each with a different opinion.

Some readers thought it was wrong for the editor to print a child's make-believe story and encourage her to continue to live in a dream world instead of growing up. Others thought Julia's story was charming, like children's dreams of Santa Claus.

A number of readers about Julia's age wrote to the paper with their own theories about where the Sea Bear had come from. Two or three of them said that they had learned the Sea Bear's secret by dreaming about him, long before Julia had touched the Sea Bear's fur in the gift shop.

One letter to the editor was framed in a black box on the first page, and that caught everyone's attention. The woman who wrote the letter was a geologist at the college in San Luis Obispo and knew all about rocks and their different formations. She also knew a lot about California earthquakes. She had read Julia's story with interest because five years ago there had been a sudden, strong quake near Blue Cove.

Back up in the mountains, where the woman often explored, she had noticed the changes the earthquake had caused. Stone pinnacles had fallen, and the ground had opened up. She was especially interested in underground caves, which she said honeycombed the whole region.

The geologist was excited and got out her maps. She drew a line eastward from the Sea Bear's beach and identified an area that resembled the large meadow in Julia's story. The meadow was next to a high wall of unsteady rocks she had observed before.

The next weekend, when she wasn't teaching, she would go into the mountains to find the wilderness area that Julia's story had made her remember.

More letters were printed in the paper. Some readers thought the geologist was crazy. Others thought it was just sad that a grown person believed the fantasy of a nine-year-old girl.

The story remained unfinished until a week later, when the geologist appeared on the TV news. She had found the meadow, the cave, and the tunnel, and had ventured inside until the fallen rubble had blocked her way. She had a video camera with her, and the TV station showed footage of the green meadow, the cave entrance, and the dim tunnel where the woman had crawled in, lighting her way with a powerful spotlight. She was sure the cave led due west to the coast, to the Sea Bear's cave and his beach.

However, to prove her theory, the rocks blocking the tunnel would have to be removed, which might be both dangerous and impossible. Her video showed how big and heavy the rocks were.

Jerry, the local reporter who had overhead Julia's story in the gift shop, located Julia's family in Florida. When he called, Julia's mother answered. She remembered the visit to the gift shop and the toy Sea Bear, which was in Julia's room, by her pillow. The mother wasn't surprised that the tunnel had been found, and that it probably led from the high forest meadow to the beach.

"What about the Sea Bear's dream?" the reporter heard Julia ask her mother.

"I don't think he can check that," her mother told Julia. "We'll just have to wait and see."

"Wait and see what?" the reporter asked.

"I don't really want to say any more," the mother answered. "Julia's had enough press coverage for now."

Meanwhile the Sea Bear had been living his regular life, not knowing about Julia or her mother or the newspapers or the geologist. Fall had arrived, and the weather was getting colder, and when he looked up at the tops of the cliffs he noticed fewer creatures looking down at him.

The Sea Bear had seen five years of seasons come and go, and he wasn't afraid that winter was coming. He was healthy and never hungry, and if he wanted he could sleep more during the winter, living off the fat he had stored up during the long warm spring and summer.

No one ever knew if the Sea Bear dreamed, or if he did what he dreamed of. Maybe he dreamed of the island, of the other bear.

...

One day the seabirds cried more loudly than usual. The passing sea otters had gone away, and the seal that the Sea Bear knew popped his sleek black head from the waves only once, then disappeared. The sky turned gray, then darker as the wind began to blow clouds to the coast from the wild sea. The Sea Bear hurried back to his cave and lay down, listening to the wind and the rain until he went to sleep.

It was one of the fiercest storms on record. Roofs were blown off houses, seaside homes were flooded by high waves, and streets along the coast were covered with mud washed down from the hillsides. Hundreds of tons of driftwood floated in, and piles fifteen feet high clogged the beaches.

Seabirds had been blown far inland by the high winds, and rangers and volunteers walked the shore, bringing exhausted and injured gulls, sandpipers, and pelicans to the emergency animal shelter.

The Sea Bear's status was unknown. After the storm, he had not been seen on the beach, and there was worry that the high tide had poured into his cave and taken him out to sea.

Hundreds of worried callers phoned the TV station, asking for news about the Sea Bear. The TV station suggested that the callers contact the rangers' station, and then the already busy rangers swooped into action.

They hurried aboard their white boat and set off up the coast in the choppy water. They drifted just offshore at the Sea Bear's beach, watching through their binoculars. No sight of the Sea Bear.

The captain ordered the rowboat to be lowered, and three rangers, two of them with rifles, rowed toward the beach where for five years no human had set foot.

The rangers ran their boat up onto the sand, looking up and down the beach, which was strewn with driftwood, but there wasn't any sign of the Sea Bear. They started for the Sea Bear's cave, not going straight toward it but walking in a wide curve, in case the Sea Bear was watching them.

The Sea Bear didn't come out of his cave as the rangers approached along the hard wet sand from the record high tide. At the dark entrance, they listened but didn't hear the Sea Bear breathing. One of them picked up a small piece of driftwood and threw it into the cave, but nothing stirred from the dark. Then one ranger took out his flashlight, and carefully the three men entered.

The cave was empty.

They saw only the Sea Bear's rumpled old blankets and a small pile of fish. They heard the bubbling water, and with the flashlight they found the Sea Bear's drinking pool.

The Sea Bear was nowhere to be found, but as they left the cave one ranger noticed something.

"Look," said the ranger, pointing to the ground. "Those are the Sea Bear's footprints."

The prints headed straight toward their boat, which was waiting for them between two high piles of driftwood.

The three rangers followed the paw prints the Sea Bear had made. One of them stopped and leaned down to touch one of the footprints.

"I didn't know he was so big," the ranger said.

About thirty yards ahead, all three rangers stopped and turned to one another, and then they walked slowly toward the branches and tree trunks washed ashore by the storm.

They looked to the left and right, sure the Sea Bear must be close by, maybe hiding among the tall stacks of driftwood, ready to spring out and attack them.

The rangers each remembered the old story about the trespassing diver in the wet suit and wondered if the Sea Bear might have eaten the frightened man if he hadn't dived into the surf before the Sea Bear could catch him.

The two rangers with rifles held their guns out straight. The guns shot darts, but the tranquilizer drug took two minutes to put a large animal into a deep sleep.

Now the Sea Bear's tracks headed straight for the sea. The rangers looked out at the waves, but they didn't see the Sea Bear.

They were almost to the edge of the lapping water when all three came to another sudden stop.

From the ocean, another set of four paw prints was imprinted onto the sand, approaching the Sea Bear's tracks. The tracks faced each other, a few feet apart, as if two animals had touched noses. And then the set of tracks from the sea turned in a circle, and the prints of all eight paws disappeared into the ocean.

One of the rangers called the captain, and before long everyone in Blue Cove knew the Sea Bear was gone. They began gathering at the cliff, watching the rangers' boat search in hopeless circles far out beyond the beach.

"Did the Sea Bear who dreamed of the bear on the island find his mate?" the editor of the newspaper wrote on the front page the next day.

The editor included in his story the news that Jerry the reporter had again called Julia's family. This time, Julia answered the phone, and Jerry told her the news about the Sea Bear and asked for her opinion.

"Yes, they're together now," Julia said. "The two bears."

"You're sure?" Jerry asked.

"Positive," said Julia. "By now they've probably reached their island."

"Well," said Jerry. "I guess that's the end of the Sea Bear's story."

"Oh no," Julia answered. "It's not. It's just the beginning."

"It is?" Jerry asked.

"Yes," said Julia. "If I didn't have to get my homework

done, I could tell you the whole story. I'm studying for a history test tomorrow. Math is easy, like tracing a picture with your pencil. History is a lot harder."

A Normal Rabbit

Rachel King

AT BREAKFAST, Allie stares out the window. She wants the sky to stop crying. Rain rivulets unite in their flow down the window. She watches patterns emerge and mindlessly spoons Raisin Bran into her mouth. Today she is going to show her rabbit, Camper, at the fair.

Her little brother, Drew, sits on his knees on the chair next to hers. He has forgotten about eating; his finger follows a maze on the back of the cereal box. Allie puts down her spoon and rubs her brother's blond buzz. He shakes her off and continues in his puzzle world.

Dad enters and closes the box. He squats to Drew's level. "We're going to the fair!" he tells him. Drew continues doing the maze. "Come help me put Camper in his box," Dad says. Drew looks at Dad when he mentions Camper. "Okay," he says, but he insists on dragging the cereal box behind him. Allie pokes around for more raisins in her lake of milk.

Last fall, a few months after they bought their first two rabbits, the family, eating dinner on the patio, heard rabbit squeals. They all ran to the rabbit hutch and saw one rabbit tearing apart beige, furless baby rabbits. The other grown-up rabbit was dead. Allie started crying. Drew stared and would have stuck his finger in the cage if Dad hadn't pulled him away. Since then, her parents are always talking about autism or Asperger's syndrome. Allie doesn't understand much but senses from her parents' tones and tenseness that something might be wrong with Drew.

On the drive to the fair, Camper sits in a large cardboard file box between Allie and Drew. Drew pets him continually. Allie looks at the raindrops on the car window. Sun shines through them now, and they glisten. When they drive over a bridge, she imagines it breaking and their car falling into the river. Climbing out the windows while the car sinks. She wonders if rabbits can swim. Drew can't. He would hold onto Camper's box, and she would hold onto him and swim them all to safety.

...

They park in a gravel lot behind a two-story white building. As soon as she steps from the car, Allie smells popcorn and cotton candy. A blue Ferris wheel peeks out from behind the building. Dad carries Camper's box, and Mom carries a red backpack containing their lunch and rain jackets, just in case. Allie takes Drew's hand. She wants to show him all the rides and animals.

They round the edge of the building, and Allie gapes at the fair. The pirate boat that rocks higher and higher until you're almost upside down. The silver roller coaster she hopes she's tall enough to ride this year. The blue-and-white stand shaped like an icy drink. The river below the fairgrounds that disappears behind a red barn. Last year she saw piglets and ponies in there.

Drew pulls away from her. He marches up and down, up and down the building's four steps.

"Come on, kids, we need to check Camper in," Mom says. Drew doesn't look at her, so she scoops him up by the armpits and lifts him up the steps. Allie jumps the steps two at a time, her brown pigtails slapping against the back of her neck.

Inside, Dad sets the box on a table. A gray-haired lady, sitting behind the table on a fold-out chair, lifts her thin body and squints into the box.

"What 4-H group?" she asks.

"South Salem," Dad says.

"We just signed up," Mom adds, "so we might not be on your list."

"Last name?" the lady asks.

"Callahan," Dad says.

"We have you," the lady says. "But it doesn't say what breed of rabbit you've got there."

Mom and Dad look at each other. Neither of them know Camper's breed. They bought him at Allie's summer camp. Camper's parents had been wild rabbits that a camp staff member tamed. The lady squints into the box again.

"It might be a dwarf of some kind," she says.

"No, he's not a dwarf," Mom says. That's the only breed of rabbit she knows. Their first two rabbits had been dwarfs of some sort—at least that's what the pet store said. Then again, they'd also told her both rabbits were boys.

"I didn't know they divided them by breed," Dad says.

"Me neither," Mom says. "I mean, I know they do at dog shows, but I thought it was more informal with rabbits. What breeds of rabbits are on your list?"

"I thought it might be a Netherland—" the lady says.

"His name's Camper," Allie says. "And he's a boy." She's not sure what *breed* means, but she doesn't want the lady to call Camper *it*.

"Honey," Mom says and shakes her head at Allie. "Maybe he *is* a Netherland."

"A Netherland's a type of dwarf," the lady says.

"Oh."

The lady taps her blue pen against the box. Dad pulls the box off the table and puts it on the tiled floor. Drew kneels and pets Camper again. Allie wants to go out to the rides. She thinks Camper's light brown fur is pretty, but ever since she saw the baby rabbit massacre, she hasn't liked to pet rabbits. That's why her parents thought showing rabbits would be good for her: She'd learn to not mind handling them. A little boy and his dad step in line behind them. The lady taps her pen against the gray plastic tabletop.

"We have lops here: Holland, English, and mini—but those rabbits have drooping ears. Its fur isn't soft enough for a rex, ears aren't long enough for a chinchilla, doesn't have the coloring of a Dutch. I'd almost say it's a Palomino—put the box up here again."

Dad sets the box back on the table. "Camper!" Drew says and punches the box's side.

"Enough, Drew," Dad says.

The lady yanks Camper up by the scruff of the neck and brings her face close to the rabbit's brown belly. "Nope," she says, dropping him back down. "Palominos have white on their belly." She looks back down at her list.

"Camper's just a normal rabbit," Allie says.

The lady squints at Allie. "I guess we have an 'other' category," she says. "We don't have any rabbits in it right now, but some people, like you, didn't list their rabbits' breeds."

"Go ahead and put Camper in that category," Dad says.

Mom squeezes her face together. "Will our daughter still be able to show him?"

"Sure," the lady says. "One o'clock, okay? You'll show upstairs. Cages are in the back of this building. Divided by breed. Put it near the Palominos, and it won't look too out of place."

"Thank you," Mom says. "We're new to the whole 4-H thing."

"You're welcome," the lady says, her eyes already questioning the next-in-line dad and son.

. . .

Last Christmas Allie's parents gave her Kit, one of the American Girl dolls. Allie's high school–age cousin gave Allie her old American Girl doll clothing and a wicker doll table and doll-size rosy pink glasses, bowls, and plates. Allie set up Kit's table next to her family's table. Every month she dressed Kit in seasonal attire: a green plaid coat and white muffler in January, a white dress covered in red hearts for February, a pink dress and frilly white pinafore for March. A stuffed monkey and teddy bear accompanied Kit at meals.

Once in a while, Drew made forts for the stuffed animals out of Lincoln Logs, but mainly he liked to watch Allie play. He stared at her while she composed dialogue for her toys. He took two Lincoln Logs and tapped them against the coffee table like drumsticks. He wore the pink glasses like thimbles over each of his thumbs. The first time Allie pulled a glass off one of his thumbs, Drew started screaming. Mom came in wearing her worried face and said that he wasn't hurting anything. "They're mine," Allie said. "You can share," Mom said. Mom didn't even make Drew apologize when he cracked one while trying to bang on the piano keys. Now the bear and monkey had to drink out of the same glass.

In the spring the doctors said Drew didn't have autism, but that he may have Asperger's syndrome; it was too soon to tell. Mom and Dad discussed his possible symptoms while they made supper. Allie listened to them from the next room, where she prepared supper for Kit and her stuffed animals.

"He colored for two hours straight today," Dad said once.

"Well, he likes that dinosaur coloring book," Mom said. "It's not unusual for a kid his age." Another time, Mom said, "Drew played with Rob today."

"Did they play together, or did Drew alternate between playing by himself and trying to talk Rob's ear off?" Dad asked.

"Don't be so pessimistic," Mom said.

Drew loved to describe to Allie all the different pictures in Richard Scarry books. Sometimes, because she wasn't interested in every part of a fire truck or a hospital, she would turn away in the middle of an explanation, and Drew would scream. Once, after such an incident, Dad knelt down on the floor by the book and said, "Listen, Allie, you need to be patient with your brother. He's a little different than—"

"We don't know that," said Mom, kneeling down, too, and looking into Allie's eyes. "You need to be patient and kind to your brother because he's your brother. You're older than him and need to take care of him."

Now, when Drew starts elaborating on pictures in books, Allie listens to him with part of her brain and uses the other part to make sure she knows how to read every word on the page.

...

They walk past black-spotted white rabbits, white-spotted black rabbits, glassy-eyed rabbits, short-eared rabbits, and lop-eared rabbits. The cages are at Allie's eye level. One large lop's bushy gray hair completely covers its eyes. Allie stops and sounds out the name of the breed, written on a white card affixed to the cage. "Angora."

"Angora." Mom places the accent on the second, not the third, syllable. "Looks like a mini-sheep, doesn't it?"

"A sheep?" Drew asks.

"I want to see the real sheep," Allie says.

"In a minute, honey," Mom says and lifts up Drew. "It's just a rabbit, honey. With real long hair. See its rabbitty ears?"

They put Camper in an empty cage in the back corner. He jumps around, kicking his hind legs, nervous. Allie stacks up some straw to make a bed for him. A staff member at summer camp told her it hurts rabbits' feet to stand on metal wire caging all day. She notices some rabbits don't have a shoebox or a bed of straw to sit on, and she feels bad for them. Dad and Drew go outside to fill up the rabbit's water bottle while Mom fills out the white card. *Name*: Camper Callahan. *Age*: 6 months. She leaves the *Breed* line blank, slips the card back into its plastic slipcover, and attaches it to the cage.

"Why didn't you write 'other' next to *Breed*?" Dad asks as he attaches the water bottle to the cage. The ball inside the water bottle's metal spout clicks quickly and noisily as Camper, trying to extract water, pushes against it with his tongue.

"That's not really a breed," Mom says. She pulls a bag of rabbit pellets from her backpack and gently siphons the pellets into a bowl through a hole in the plastic. "Camper might have a breed. That lady didn't sound like she knew what she was talking about." She places the bowl in the cage.

"She sounded like she knew exactly what she was talking about," Dad says. He hoists Drew onto his shoulders. Drew pounds on Dad's black Beavers cap with the butt of his fists, and Dad winces as the metal button on top pushes into his head. Camper uses his hind legs to kick straw into the air. "Who's up for some kettle corn?" Dad asks.

"Me! Me!" Allie says.

"It's ten o'clock in the morning," Mom says.

"Exactly." Dad winks at Mom, and she smiles.

"Oh, all right. We don't go to the fair every day."

...

The bag of kettle corn, stood upright, comes up to Drew's nose. Dad says they can only eat it down to Drew's belly button before lunch. Allie plays with the sugar crystals on her tongue and, later, to ward off nervousness, picks at the kernels in her teeth while waiting for the roller coaster to start. Drew seems to like the Ferris wheel. Allie points out their car to him, and the building that holds Camper. He starts running in circles when she tries to show him the barn animals, so Dad takes him out by the river to eat a peanut butter and jelly sandwich. While Mom and Allie eat lunch, Drew stacks up a pile of sticks and proposes lighting them on fire. Then it's time to show Camper.

People and rabbits fill the second floor. Families sit in lawn chairs or on blankets and eat their lunches and chat with one another. Along three walls run foldout tables, above which hang numbered posters detailing the names and pictures of each rabbit breed. Allie and her family stand at the large room's entrance. They don't recognize anyone. Mom calls her 4-H contact, and soon a heavy-set, middle-age man in a yellow Ducks cap comes to greet them.

"There's always a few rabbits in the 'other' category," the man says after Mom explains the situation. "Don't worry about it. Come join the group."

Mom's about to ask another question, but Dad makes a crack about the Ducks, and the two men start discussing Pac-12 football. As they huddle into the corner of a large burgundy blanket, a bullhorn announces that anyone with mini-lops should bring them to table seven. A curly-haired redhead next to Allie stands up, a white-and-beige rabbit in her arms. "Feel her ears," she tells Allie. "They're real soft."

Allie feels the ears, which are twice as long as the rabbit's head. "Yeah, they are soft," she says. Inside one ear, her finger halts on bumps that feel like the braille on the outside of restaurant bathroom doors. "What's that?" Allie asks the girl.

The girl opens the ear fold, and Allie reads numbers: 3218. "Her tattoo," the girl says. "Doesn't yours have one?" She walks away, both arms curled underneath and around her large rabbit.

Allie bends over Camper's box. Camper is scrunched into the corner, shaking, his brown eyes bulging. Drew balls up the fur around Camper's neck and releases it, over and over again. Allie examines the insides of Camper's ears. They are white and pink and covered in veins, and she doesn't see or feel a tattoo anywhere.

"All the 4-Hers who registered their rabbits in the 'other' category, please proceed to table eleven," the bullhorn says.

"I suppose that's us," Mom says.

Allie lifts up Camper.

"Where's Camper going?" Drew asks.

"You can come with me," Allie tells him.

"Just do what the judge with the clipboard tells you," the man in the Ducks cap says. "You'll do great."

"Come watch Drew so I can take a picture of Allie," Mom tells Dad.

"Okay," Dad says.

Allie feels Camper shaking against her chest. She steps over blankets and kids' legs and blue coolers and brown paper sacks. Her table is the only one without a picture above it. Three other kids and their rabbits stand behind the table. A woman wearing thick glasses and a sequined purple cap and carrying a clipboard examines one rabbit. Mom takes Allie's picture while she waits her turn.

"What a beautiful buck," the lady says when she steps across from Allie. Allie smiles. At least this lady knows Camper is a boy. "His front and back feet line up." The lady marks something on her clipboard and then examines Camper's teeth and eyes. "He doesn't have sniffles, and his eyes are clean." She marks something else and then opens his ears. "His ears are clean. But where's his number, dear?"

"He ... he doesn't have one," Allie says.

"Is this your first show?"

"Yes."

"And no one told you he needed a number? It's the rules. He needs a number to qualify for a prize. I'd like to give your rabbit a ribbon, dear, but you need to get him a tattoo first. See that square card table in the corner?"

Allie nods.

Mom steps up. "What's the tattoo for?"

"It's an identifying number," the lady says. "All show rabbits need them. A 4-H rule."

"Does it hurt them?"

"Not any more than getting your ears pierced." She lowers her voice. "This rabbit is the most well-formed mutt here. Go get him a tattoo, and your rabbit gets a ribbon. Might even have a shot at best-in-show."

Mom nods. "You finished looking him over?"

"One moment," she says. She feels his fur and then lifts him up by the scruff of the neck and examines his stomach. His hind legs bounce downward and back toward his bottom. His body slides as she sets him back down on the plastic. "Okay, go ahead and take him. Report back to me with the tattoo number."

"Okay," Mom says. "Come on, Allie. Bring Camper over here."

A teenage girl and guy stand behind the tattoo table. A fur-covered raggedy green towel is on top of the table, along with a box of Kleenex, a bottle of alcohol, a plastic baggie full of cotton balls, a bottle of black ink, and a metal clamp. Drew reaches toward the clamp; it looks like the toy he uses to make noodles out of Play-Doh.

"Need a tattoo?" asks the guy, pulling the clamp out of Drew's reach. Dad squats down and places Drew on his knee. Allie sets Camper on the green towel.

"Yes," Mom says.

"Is 7843 an okay number?" the guy asks, looking down at a list of typed numbers.

"Does it make a difference?" Mom asks.

"Just has to be a unique tattoo. Come hold it," he tells the girl next to him. She wraps Camper in the towel and firmly holds him with both her hands. Drew's eyes widen as he stares up at the rabbit. While the guy cleans out Camper's ear with an alcohol-soaked cotton ball, Drew whimpers. "They're hurting Camper," he says.

"Camper's going to be fine," Dad says and squeezes Drew's shoulders.

The guy places Camper's left ear inside the clamp, and Camper squeals and twists his body around. Allie hasn't heard a rabbit squeal since last fall. She tenses and bites her lip until it draws blood. Drew screams, very loudly. Half the people in the room stop their business and turn toward them.

"Jesus," the guy says. "Can you take that kid out of here?"

Drew wails even louder. "They're hurting Camper, they're hurting Camper!" he yells over and over again.

"I'll take him outside," Dad tells Mom.

"Please," Mom says. "Go ahead."

Allie thinks Mom should be upset, as she was at Allie's fifth birthday when Allie made a huge scene because she didn't get the corner, frosting-lathered piece of cake she wanted. Then Mom had spanked her. Now she looks happy.

The guy adjusts the clamp, and Mom steps forward. "I

changed my mind," she says. "We're not going to get the tattoo today. Thanks anyway."

"Your rabbit has to have the tattoo if you want it to compete," the guy says.

"I know," Mom says. "We might get it another day."

The girl relaxes her grip.

"Allie, put Camper in the box. We're going home."

Camper's hind legs twitch spasmodically as Allie places him on a pile of straw. Mom, beaming, lifts up the box. Allie follows her downstairs. They find Dad leaning against the bumper of their car, munching on kettle corn. Drew's wailing flows out of the open car door. Mom shoves Camper's box in the car and crawls inside to comfort Drew. His crying subsides. Dad holds out the bag of popcorn to Allie, and she scoops up a handful.

"You know," Dad says in between bites, when Mom emerges from the car, "that's the first time Drew has voiced empathy."

"I know," Mom says. Her eyes are red as if she, too, has been crying.

"Now that doesn't prove anything for sure—" Dad says.

"Okay, Mr. Optimistic," Mom says. "Let's go home."

"It's a good sign," Dad says. "I'll admit that. Hey, isn't Allie going to see if she won anything?"

"Not today," Mom says. "We'll come to another show. You want to, Allie?"

"Yeah," Allie says. "Maybe." Rabbit fur and popcorn mix together in her mouth, and she wonders whether to savor the tastes or spit them out. "Rabbit shows are fun."

"Did you hear the lady say Camper had a shot at best-in-show?" Mom asks Dad.

Allie spits into a puddle.

"No," Dad says. "That's great. I guess we got a good rabbit. But I'm ready to call it a day, too." Allie grabs another handful of popcorn. "Hey, save some of that for me, kiddo."

When they get in the car, Drew is asleep, his head tilted to one side, his hand clutching the fur on Camper's back. Allie feels Camper's stomach. He has stopped shaking.

As they drive home, fog rises, and Allie can't see the river water when they cross the bridge. She pretends the bridge is the drawbridge to their castle. Mom and Dad are queen and king, she and Drew are princess and prince. Camper is the royal rabbit. Tonight she and Drew will take him to supper at the wicker table and introduce him to Kit, her teddy bear, and her monkey.

A Sterile Place

Catherine Evleshin

FROM MY WINDOW, I stare out into the marsh, looking for trees big enough to climb, but I see only dead stumps and gravel paths that snake around clumps of cattails. I have lived so long that the skin on my knuckles is transparent. Not much left of me but bones. I live in a sterile place where they call me Bob. I don't know if that's my name. I can't hear very well, even with those squawky things they put in my ears so they can shout, "Eat your dinner, Bob," or "Be a good boy, Bob, and swallow your meds."

People say that we are in the middle of the twenty-first century. I don't remember much, but they tell me I'm older than everyone here. A lot of them must be pretty old because they have transparent knuckles like mine.

One day everyone gathered in the room where we eat, and a caregiver wheeled me up to a table where a big cake sat covered with candles. They told me I had lived a century, all the way back to the time when the whole world was at war, and lucky to be a small boy who didn't have to go and get himself killed. I recall the nights my parents sat around

153

a wooden box and listened to a man talk about millions of deaths. There must have been a lot of people who didn't die because I don't remember a time when there weren't plenty of us around. But then, I get confused sometimes.

The sterile place has a garden where I sit on sunny afternoons. When it hasn't rained for a while and the river is low, the boy who calls me Great-grandpa wheels my chair down into the marsh, along the gravel paths that meander through the reeds. He sets the brake so the chair can't slip off into the mud. In the quiet I turn on those things in my ears and hear air bubbles popping out of the slime and insects rubbing their legs together like miniature violinists. A black bird with a red spot on his wing clings to a reed and cries for a mate.

During storms, the water rises and covers the paths. On those days, the boy doesn't come, so I can't visit the marsh. He says the electric sky could burn out what little is left of my brain, and the river might carry me away. When the fog lifts from my mind, I talk to one of the computers. Words appear on the screen, and when I'm finished, a caregiver sends them to the boy.

One day when the boy visited, he said, "Great-grandpa, you wrote a lotta weird stuff last week. You talked about going to war against an army of worms." We both laugh, but I'm not laughing inside.

That got me thinking back to the days when I lived with my family in a house at the edge of our fields of alfalfa. I would climb trees near the house and pull plums from the branches. They tasted good. Up high like that, I could see across the fields and think about what I was going to do when I grew up.

When I walked through the field in front of the house, I would see a row of birds sitting along the wire fence. They didn't scatter unless I got too close. Butterflies—white, yellow, and orange—flapped and glided through the air and sometimes caught a ride on my shoulder. I heard bugs go silent until I got past them, and then they would start up again, all talking at once, like the people in the sterile place.

The trees that grew on the far side of the fields were the best to climb to watch the creatures in the pond. Fish no bigger than my fingernail swam with their brothers and sisters, all turning at the same time. They never bumped into each other. On hot days, insects with transparent blue wings darted back and forth and mated in midair. I think they were called dragons.

I could hear all sorts of things back then—small birds that sang until they found a mate, then stopped singing and flitted back and forth to their nests feeding the chicks. Giant birds floated on the surface of the pond that reflected clouds overhead. They honked like the cars passing on the road. The only time the creatures in the pond fell silent was when an airplane flew overhead. That didn't happen very often.

A fat muskrat got so tame, he would swim close and look up at me standing on a limb. I would talk to him. "Hi there, friend. What are you up to today?" I guess we didn't speak the same language. After staring at me with shiny black eyes, he would dive and swim off into deep water.

Along the shallow edges of the pond, I could make out dozens of frogs half-buried in the silt at the bottom. When they got tired of holding their breath, they would swim up and sit out of the water with their eyes bulging. They had soft bellies and no hair, sort of like me, but when they stretched and doubled their long legs, they swam like they owned the water. Every now and then, one of them would let out a croak, jump with its legs and big feet flapping the air, and land in the water with a splash. It made me laugh.

When the sun disappeared behind the hills to the west, they talked to each other, bullfrogs in deep tones and their little sisters in high-pitched squeaks, a rhythm that started me bouncing up and down. One time the branch broke, and I landed on the ground. They stopped talking long enough to see that I was okay, then took up their chorus again.

When I go down to the marsh, I look hard for those fat little frogs. I want to show them to the boy, but all I see are crawly things that look like overgrown bugs. The boy calls them land crabs. They don't jump or talk.

Once when the boy visited me, he brought me words written on a stack of square leaves stuck together along one side. He said I wrote those words a long time ago, before he was born, when everyone wrote on square leaves. "Look, Great-grandpa. Your name, right on the cover." The words made no sense, but I didn't want to ask him to read my own name to me.

He wheeled me into a big closet filled with rows of square leaves crammed on dusty shelves. I smelled mold, and the boy sneezed. "They're called books, Great-grandpa. Don't you remember? You wrote a bunch of 'em about the wars."

I can't even write my name now, if I knew what it was. He says: No problem; the computer hears everything and nobody reads books anymore, except on the Internet—whatever that is.

The musty stacks of square leaves in that closet got me to thinking again about the year the army worms attacked the alfalfa. My father said they weren't really worms because they changed into butterflies. Most years, a few of the little black crawlers hid in the alfalfa plants, and no one paid much attention to them.

But that year they lived up to their name. From out of nowhere, thousands of them inched across the asphalt road that led to town and headed toward us like invading troops. My father looked worried and gripped our heavy black phone in his hand. After talking a long time, he hung the phone on the wall and patted my head. "Everything will be all right."

After lunch, he told us to stay inside. He stuffed a blue

bandanna into his shirt pocket and left the house. It was a hot afternoon, and my sister and I wanted to go outside and run through the sprinklers, but my mother said, "Not today. It's going to be dangerous out there." She locked all the windows tight. I knew something important was about to happen because she let us eat cookies before dinner.

We sat at the kitchen table and dunked cookies in cold milk while she read *The Wind in the Willows* to us. I heard the roar of an airplane overhead, so loud it drowned out our mother's voice, and I shouted, "We're in a war!"

My sister and I ran to peek through the lace curtains. The plane just missed the roof of our house. With the bandanna tied over his nose and mouth, my father stood at the edge of the field, waving a red flag. The plane headed straight toward him, and my sister screamed. He ducked just as it reached the edge of the field. I thought the plane would crash, but the pilot must have been good because he flew straight down the field just a few feet above the alfalfa plants.

Suddenly a white mist shot out of the wings, and I remembered back during the war, when every night the voice in the wooden box told about things dropping from planes to kill people. The pilot flew the length of the field, the white mist stopped, and the plane rose into the air just in time to miss the tops of the trees. I was glad when it disappeared and that awful noise faded in the distance. My sister wrinkled her nose. "What's that stinky smell?"

My father walked about thirty feet along the edge of the field and looked across to the other side. The airplane appeared over the tops of the trees and dipped down into the field again, the white spray pouring from the wings, and all the while my father flapped that red flag like crazy. The plane was now headed straight toward our house. The windows rattled as it zoomed over the roof. I saw the frown on my mother's face, but she said, "It's okay. We're not in a war." Twice, I thought the plane was gone for good, but it returned with more white spray.

This went on until the trees grew long shadows as the sun crept toward the hills to the west. The sound faded, and I heard my father's footsteps on the path to the back door. When he opened it, his clothes hung damp and his hat brim sagged into his face. He cleared his throat and spat into the dirt at the side of the door. My mother brought him a bathrobe so he could leave his clothes outside. He smelled horrible, and my sister gagged. He disappeared into the bathroom, and I heard the shower running for a long time.

The next morning my father started out to the fields, and I asked if I could go with him. He made a face like he didn't want me along. He usually liked it when we walked out together. It was already getting hot, but he told me to put on my winter pants, thick socks, and canvas shoes. On the way out the door, he tied a clean handkerchief over my nose and mouth. "Is the plane coming back?" I asked.

He smiled without showing his teeth. "Not today." When we got to the field in front of the house, he held my hand and told me not to touch anything. He looked hard at the alfalfa plants that stood tall as my chin. "Do you see any worms moving?"

I saw lots of them dead and shriveled. My father and I stood still for a long time, listening for sounds. The butterflies were gone, and not a single bird sat on the wire fence. Silence, like I'd never heard before. My father's face became a map of lines.

We walked down to the pond. The flying dragons were gone, and no fat little frogs poked their eyes out of the water. The muskrat swam up to look around, then dived and disappeared. We headed back to the house.

Years later, I got a call from my mother to say that my father had died. "He's out of his suffering." He'd fought cancer for years.

Last week, the boy who calls me Great-grandpa wheeled us down along the path through the marsh, and once again, I looked hard for the fat frogs, but all I saw were overgrown bugs and the black bird with a red spot on his wing. He still hasn't found a mate.

In the sterile place, I watch the big screen in the room where we eat dinner. They always turn down the sound, but one night I saw dozens of children who looked like skeletons. I guess they have nothing to eat where they live. An old woman behind me complained, so the caregiver changed the picture to one that showed a whole screen full of trees that stood twenty times taller than a man. Their twigs looked brown and shriveled, like the dead worms in my father's field.

Today the boy arrived carrying a square gadget. "Great-grandpa, I told my teacher about the messages you send me, and she said our class could make a collection of stories to put on the Internet." He held up the device and pointed to its small screen. "If you tell me a story, I'll put it in the book."

I rub my transparent knuckles, and the fog lifts from my brain. "When I was a boy, I lived near a pond filled with birds and fish and a muskrat and ... " I glance out the window at the marsh. "Frogs."

The boy looks confused, and so I spell it out for him. "F-r-o-g-s."

"Were they like little dinosaurs, Great-grandpa?"

"In a way. They were my friends."

The boy studies the word on the screen. "Go on, Great-grandpa."

"One year, millions of worms crossed the road and attacked my father's alfalfa fields like an invading army ... "

How to Identify Birds in the Wild

Robyn Ryle

1. Size

ROSE HAS NEVER HELD a mourning dove in her hand, but she knows it would be smaller than it looks. Birds are always smaller than you think. She held a sparrow in her hand and watched it shrink in size. She felt it flutter against her fingers before she wrapped the metal band around its tiny leg.

The mourning doves move like pigeons. They perch together on the power line above the street in the morning. She hears them everywhere she goes, the call she mistook for an owl when she was young. In her mind, the *coo-coo* of a mourning dove is what an owl should sound like.

From Manuel's window, they are at eye level. "Eye ring," she whispers at them. "Wing spots. Tail tip." She loves the soft white of their underbelly when their feathers are ruffled. The way the black wing stripes cut across the smooth buff of their body. If you look long enough, there is something beautiful about every bird.

2. Maturity

Rose hates the sound the empty bottles make clinking against the hard concrete of the curb. She hates the way Manuel tries to pick up all the bags at once so that he can do this chore alone. Without her. The way he doesn't look at her, only the bags, and the look says everything. Because he carries too many, he drops one against the sidewalk, and a bottle breaks. Rose imagines eyes looking out of the dark windows all around her on the street: Who are those kids, and why are they making so much noise?

She hates that she is twenty-three and still sharing a house with ten other people. She hates the way the house smells, like sweat and beer and shoes.

3. Nesting behavior

The house they rent is old, tucked in among other old houses in a town Rose sometimes cannot believe exists. The floors are hardwood, and the ceilings are fifteen feet high. The woman who lives in the house the rest of the year is a florist, and the windows are filled with plants that climb up toward the ceilings. When Rose sits in the living room, looking out through the leaves, sometimes she feels as if she never leaves the woods at all. She searches the branches for Henslow sparrows. She sees them when she closes her eyes at night. Sometimes Manuel's eyes in the dark beside her become black and tiny, like a bird's. His motions sharp and distinct, like the sparrow raising its head in alarm and freezing at her approach.

As she lies in the large poster bed and waits for Manuel to make his way from his room to hers, she can see down into the first-floor window of the house across the street. In this town, no one draws their blinds. At night, the neighbors pull closed shutters on the lower half of the window and leave the top half open. The windows run the length of the wall, and at night you can see inside their houses as if they are long, living TV screens.

Across the street, there's a red couch. A woman and a man. A small girl. At night, they sit on the couch, bathed in the bluish light from a TV screen.

"That's rude, to watch them through the window like that," Manuel says when she shows him the couch and the window.

But it is a pleasure Rose cannot resist.

4. Native range

On the third day of the count, Rose stands in the bathroom on the second floor, braiding her long, red hair into two pigtails. She opens the medicine cabinet door, and as the mirror tilts, she has a view of a small house on a hill in a clearing of trees. She looks out the window, but she can't see the house. It's there in the mirror but not out the window. A trick of light and angle.

"That's Kentucky across the river," she says to Manuel. "We can see two states from the bathroom."

"That's the South over there," he says. He doesn't even bother to look.

5. Habitat

For the first week, it is still cool at the site in the morning. When she comes home in the afternoon, it is only dirt she needs to shower off. No sweat. Her legs below the knee are crisscrossed with tiny scratches from the weeds and branches, but she has no memory of how each happened. Sometimes, they bleed.

Then it is hot all day long. Hot in the morning. Hotter in the afternoon. They turn the air conditioning in the old house on high. Marne laughs and says that she could hear the sound of it rumbling from blocks away. She shows Rose the goosebumps that rise on her arm when they walk in the front door of the house.

It is always cooler in the woods, though. Even in the hottest part of the day.

"It's the darker green," she tells Manuel. "It makes it feel cool."

"It's the shade."

One day they find a place so far inside the leaves they cannot tell if the sun is shining or not.

"I want you," Manuel whispers.

He presses her against a tree, and the binoculars slung around their necks bang into each other. A nuthatch freezes on the bark of a tree above them and watches, suspended upside down.

6. Vocalizations

After they've been there a month, Marne perfects her impersonation of the morning DJ on the local radio station. His words are slurred, as if he is drunk at six in the morning. There are long pauses in the middle of his sentences. He sounds as if he is reading off a card, but the sentences are assembled strangely, his own arrangement of verbs and nouns.

"Come on down today," Marne says. "To the riverfront." In the long pause, everyone laughs except Manuel because Manuel finds nothing amusing. "A festival. Ten dollars. At the gate. Much fun is down here, folks. Much fun."

"Should we go?" she whispers to Manuel as they take the path into the grassland. He is shorter than she is. When he moves away, he becomes a dark shape moving just above the top of the grass.

"You and Marne go," he says.

7. Field marks

What does he imagine will happen if he goes to the festival? If he goes out into the town? She asks him over and over. What would they do? What would they say?

"Nothing, probably."

"Then why can't we go? Why can't you go? I want to be places with you. I want to hold your hand. I want to sit in the grass and listen to music."

"Why?" he asks. "Why do you want those things?"

"Why don't you?"

It's not the girlfriend. No one here knows about the girlfriend. No one knows anything about Manuel but his name. Sometimes Marne asks, and Rose just shakes her head. She keeps every small detail about Manuel to herself. She hoards them away under the bed. She cups them in her hand, and each one appears so small.

On the morning after he tells her he won't be coming to her bed at night anymore, she wakes with cramps. Her organs are coiled tight and twisted around each other inside. She cannot eat. Cannot talk. She rides in the van in silence and she sees a cut-out portion of Manuel's face in the rearview mirror as he drives.

"Eye ring. Wing spots. Tail tip," she whispers.

8. Species status

In the woods, she can barely stand up straight, so great is the pain.

"Do you want some Advil?" Marne asks.

But there are no pills for this pain.

She sits down in the cool waters of the little creek. She hangs her head. She imagines her body dissolving, each bit of her floating away downstream.

A cloud passes over, and the light where she sits fades. It grows darker and darker, and she is alone. Marne is somewhere downstream, but in the gloom, Rose thinks there is someone there. Someone in the woods with her. A figure behind the largest tree. Someone who knows the hidden location of all the birds. Someone who watches Rose through their eyes.

She lies back in the stream and lets the current tug at her hair. The crawfish crawl between her fingers.

9. Migration patterns

She has to take one of the vans home by herself because the pain is too much. For the first time, she has the house all to herself. Her footsteps echo through the open spaces and catch in the branches of the plants. There is no other noise to steal the sound away. No voices. No music. She discovers places where the floorboards creak.

She smells the air for the first time—the staleness of the air conditioning—and she opens a window. The hot air rushes inside.

It is too cold. She is feverish. She takes a beer from the fridge for painkiller and goes out on the front porch. The mourning doves are not there. They will appear again in the evening at the same time the chimney swallows begin to gather.

10. Flight patterns

"Are you one of the bird people?"

A woman stands on the street beside the porch. She wears a vintage T-shirt that's tight across her large breasts and flabby arms. Her face is familiar, but Rose can't remember how.

"Sorry?"

"Are you one of the bird people? From the university? Jenny told us she rented out to some students who were here to watch the birds." It is the woman from across the street. The one who sits on her red couch in the evening.

"Count them. We're here to count them."

"You're usually not back this early." She looks at the street where all the vehicles would be lined up by afternoon. She looks at Rose's beer. "Everything okay?"

Rose is nothing without him because difference defines everything. The eyes of the Cooper's hawk are closer to the front of the head than those of the sharp-shinned hawk. The downy woodpecker's bill is small relative to its head, while the hairy woodpecker's bill is long and thick. House finches are more slender than purple finches. When she finds his hairs scattered on the pillow, they are straight black pins while hers are bright red commas.

She looks at the woman standing on the sidewalk in front of her and then stares up at the power line, waiting for the mourning doves to return.

The woman in the street waits for Rose to answer. She shifts back and forth in her comfortable shoes.

"Everything's fine," Rose says.

11. Silhouette

A picture of their two bodies from above in the big poster bed at night. They would be outlined by that rectangle. A poster of the twists and turns of their bodies entwined. Every night when he crawled into her bed, this is what she imagined. A large camera above that caught the contrast of her white skin and his darker. Her red hair, his black. Her arm thrown across his chest. His leg angled out away from her, pointing toward the door.

She imagined an entire art exhibit of people in their beds photographed from above. The way they moved at night. Touching or not. Huddling together or assigned to far sides of the bed with blankets for boundaries. They would flash like a time-lapse series. She had seen such images used to reveal how active we are in our sleep. The hidden motions of the night.

In the pictures of her and Manuel, she would be alone in

the first frame. He would appear in the fourth. In the fifth he would draw close, the ecstatic greeting. In the eighth, he would pull away again. He suffered from insomnia. He would toss and turn beside Rose. He would not turn to her for comfort.

In some of the frames, though, they would be beautiful together. She imagined the pictures in black and white. The soft surface of Manuel's stomach. His dark eyelashes as he stared out the window. Out the door. Away from Rose.

In the last three frames, he would be gone. She would be asleep and alone. The pictures would be all she had.

Strays

Anne Elliott

THEY MADE WILD LITTLE BABIES with dripping eyes and bellies bloated with worms. Many were not even cute. Some dropped hefty, inbred litters, with markings so alike they looked like a single being, a furry amoeba throbbing around the water bowl. Some staged midnight gang wars in between the fence posts and parked cars. Some had lost eyeballs or hunks of fur and tail, or had oozing abscesses on their necks, pink holes of stinking goop. Some hunched alone on stone ledges, with paws curled under and perpetual hollow looks, disappointment set in deep. Others arched and emanated anger. Maybe they had good reason.

They all hollered after the door snapped shut. They seemed to be yelling at themselves, for yielding to curiosity, for heavy-stepping, for hatch-tripping, just for that sniff of sardine.

The sardines were on cheap paper cocktail plates. Lou baited in an assembly line, like cater-waitering, only everything cheap. The sardines were cheap. The bleach she used to prep the cages was cheap. The kibble she withheld for a week to

169

starve them out was cheap. She covered each trap with an old bed sheet—also cheap—to mellow the beasts. They preferred the dark and enclosed. The only way to stop the whining was to toss a curtain over the cage. That's all, folks. Shut up and sniff your fish.

Her landlady let her shelter the cats in the basement, before and after surgery, in the room between the garbage and the laundry. There were rat traps down there, the black and sinister kind, opaque so you don't have to see whose life you've just stopped. So the rats can't warn each other of the ruse. Permanent curtain. And mousetraps, too, the sticky kind, the kind that sickened Lou with their efficiency. The landlady didn't bother to cover the mousetraps. The mice were too dumb. They became their own bait. They would see their brothers stuck and squirming out of their own fur and come over to see what the fuss was.

"Just like people," said the landlady. "They see somebody stuck someplace, they want to get stuck there, too."

The other tenants blamed Lou for the rat problem and the mouse problem and probably other problems, too. She saw their slitty-eyed looks. The thin-lipped, fakey smiles on the stairway. *Crazy cat lady is making them all multiply, all of the vermin. I even saw a raccoon! In Brooklyn!* The whispers, stopping suddenly, when she set a bowl of cheap kibble on the stoop.

Never feed a stray cat, Mother used to say. *They talk. They invite the whole army.*

Mother was dead now, and this army was starving. "I didn't give birth to them," Lou said under her breath to the un-neighborly neighbors. "I didn't dump them here."

The landlady was better. "Don't ask me for money because I'm not giving you any," she said. "Those veterinaries just want to get in your pocket."

"Not asking for donations. Except the basement space.

Just for a week. I can probably get you a tax receipt even, if you want."

"Well, since you put it that way."

"Our nighttime opera will be gone."

"They've been screaming back there since I was this big."

"So you'll miss it, then."

The landlady laughed, slowly, thoughtfully, silently, the way she did. "I just might."

. . .

Impossible not to name the critters, if only to keep them apart. Here in the basement were Stan and Rodney and Edith and Gladys, names Lou had gleaned from the cemetery across the street, where the cats courted. Also in the basement: Ariel, Simba, Pocahontas, and Nemo, named by Dwayne Junior, the landlady's grandson, who was too old to watch cartoons but did, compulsively, up in the landlady's apartment. He was another condition of the basement. The landlady wanted him to get out, broaden his vocabulary beyond the talking box in his room. He took an interest in the cats. He was the kind of kid who latched onto things. Not people so much—just things. He didn't make eye contact. Lou decided she could get used to it. The cats didn't make eye contact either.

Dwayne Junior was big for his age, which added to the mystery of his tics. Nearly diabetic, the landlady confessed, at a loss for getting vegetables in. Starchy staples were what he loved, and salty crunchy things in noisy bags. "I don't *buy* chips, Lou," said the landlady. "I don't know how they get in his hands. I don't think I *want to know* how they get in his hands."

It took a few days to fill all of the traps, and the most gullible—or desperate—cats had to cool their heels in the

171

basement and wait for the crafty ones to get caught. In the meantime, Lou and Dwayne Junior went down a couple times a day to dish out food and clean up poop in the traps.

"I have an idea," Dwayne Junior said on the second day of cat storage. "We should have two sets of food and water bowls for each cage. We can get everything ready over here first. Like a kit."

He laid out a sample kit very carefully: right angles, newspaper collated, plastic water bowl, paper dish of kibble.

"Dwayne Junior, that looks like a cafeteria tray."

"Not really. Cafeteria trays are made of plastic. And people don't eat cat food. And we drink out of cups, not bowls. And we use knives and forks. And the cats don't use napkins. A cafeteria tray would have napkins."

Dwayne Junior didn't take big leaps, she noted. It was a metaphor-free zone, this basement, among the dormant bassinets and bicycles, the recycle bins, the doomed mice, the dingy windows, the dusty steam pipes, the tenants' curious children peeking in on their way to the laundry room, tagging behind bedraggled moms. The kids didn't step into the cat room. They had been warned.

Lou helped Dwayne Junior set up cat cafeteria trays and tried to follow his design. Still, he corrected her: "The water is too close to the food." She obeyed him. She was not sure if obeying was the right thing to do. She wanted a manual for this kid.

She folded the first sheet halfway back. Pocahontas tucked herself into the covered part, the dark and enclosed. Lou stuck large combs through the halfway mark, to trap the cat in the back. She pulled out the soiled newspaper. Some cats would shred the paper to cover their smelly inevitabilities. Some, like Pocahontas, just shat neatly in the corner of the cage and let the smell waft on up, as if to say: Look what you made me do.

Lou put new paper in, closed the cage, removed the

combs, folded the sheet back over the clean end of the cage. Pocahontas migrated, and Lou reinserted the combs, then opened the other end of the cage and readied it for Dwayne Junior to insert the tray. He placed it carefully. She secured the hatch. Dwayne Junior removed the combs and replaced the sheet. "Shhh," he said to Lou, though he didn't have to. This was the best part: listening to the crunch of kibble.

"Can I do the next one? I know how to do it. I was watching you."

"Are you sure?"

Of course *he* was sure.

What the hell. She nodded. "Just don't stick your fingers in." Lou had heard stories from the queue at the mobile clinic, the parade of cat ladies and their covered cages. One volunteer had been bitten on her thumb and lost half her arm to infection. A cat's mouth was full of the unthinkable.

"I won't," he said. He was already kneeling on the floor in front of Gladys. Lou fought the urge to talk him through it. She had a feeling he didn't like to be told what to do. He followed her steps exactly, as if he had a checklist: sheet, combs, door, newspaper, door, combs, sheet. Other end. Sheet, combs, door, food tray, door, combs, then he stopped before dropping the curtain. "I think Gladys is purring. Shhh. Listen." He put his ear close to the cage.

"Careful, D. He might bite."

"*She*. This is Gladys."

"*She* might bite."

"She won't bite. She's happy. Look. She likes it in this cage."

Lou knelt next to Dwayne Junior and put her ear to the cage. Gladys flopped onto her side on the clean newspaper, pushing her tangerine fur through the wire mesh.

"Hey, Miss Lou, you're not supposed to put your fingers in the cage."

She had done it without thinking. Gladys purred and pushed against Lou's finger, relishing the scratch. She extended a paw in the air of her cage, stretching her pink toes apart. She was fat and happy and wrongly friendly.

"See, I told you. She likes it in there."

This was a cat who had hidden behind gravestones at dinnertime, always out of human reach. "Maybe she's more pregnant than I thought," Lou said.

"You mean more kittens inside?"

"I mean further along. She might be fixing to give birth right there. I hope she can hold off."

"I don't. I could keep them in my room."

"That would be up to your gran."

"I could keep them all in a cage, in my room."

"Cats don't like to be in cages, Dwayne Junior, not usually. And it's hard on them, being mothers. They don't get to eat for themselves."

"Like Ceres."

"Like Ceres." They had caught Ceres every night this week and let her go every night, after her fill of bait. Her teats dangled almost to the pavement, and her hip bones stuck out. Lou had no idea where she was hiding her kittens, only that they were killing her. They were probably fat, cute, and ungrateful. She wanted to get Ceres in for surgery, but a lactating queen would be refused.

"Can I clean the next one?" Dwayne Junior asked.

"You can do all of them, if you want."

"Really?"

The landlady dropped by about halfway through the process. "Is Junior wearing out his welcome yet?"

"Not even. He's great. Look. He's got the system down."

"Mmm." The landlady leaned against the doorjamb with her hands in the pockets of her faded yellow smock. "It's nice to see him actually doing something."

"My mother would say we are crazy, doing this."

"Don't worry, I won't tell her."

"She's not available to tell."

The landlady blushed. "Oh, I'm so sorry."

"Don't be. I think she's better off." Lou thought of the hospice nurse, the glass drip bottles of mercy. The look on Mother's face when offered a can of Ensure, that sneer at the straw under her nose. Then the other look, the look when that glass bottle was suspended overhead and plugged into her arm. Mother's jaw unclenched, and the fear left her eyes. Not food. Not what she needed.

"I got a baked ziti upstairs if you're hungry. When you two are finished."

. . .

The landlady's apartment was laid out just like Lou's but was stuffed to the gills with stuff. Two sofas in the front room, where Lou had only a chair; pictures hanging in a hodgepodge over the inert fireplace; refrigerator covered in souvenir magnets shaped like state maps and state birds. Everything was clean.

Dwayne Junior took his plate down the hall, and a Looney Tunes theme arose from his room. "He's an interesting person," Lou said.

"Thanks for noticing. Most people see him as my cross to bear."

"He's kind of fun if you just let him be." Lou accepted a paper plate of ziti and sat at the kitchen table. It was clear the landlady usually sat here alone. There was a stack of magazines next to her place mat, shouting important news of celebrity divorce, with a TV remote control parked on top. Next to the entertainment supplies was a salt and pepper set, in the shape of Bo Peep and a straggler sheep. Both figures faced Lou, who sat in the only kitchen chair.

The landlady went into the other room for a second chair. "It doesn't have meat in it," she shouted through the archway, "but that's real cheese."

"Don't worry. I'm not vegetarian."

"I thought all you animal people were vegetarians."

"Not this animal person."

The landlady sat across from her with a much smaller portion. The pasta was chewy, not overdone, and there were chunks of homegrown tomato. The cheese stretched from the plate to Lou's mouth. She had trouble breaking the strand with her fork. "I need scissors," she said through her bite of food. The landlady nodded, accepting the compliment. "Miles beyond my mother's ziti."

"You miss her cooking?"

"She didn't enjoy doing it."

"You have to enjoy it. Or it won't taste any good. Me, I don't enjoy dishes." The landlady tapped her plastic fork against the rim of her paper plate.

"She didn't enjoy much, I guess."

"That's sad. You miss her?"

"Not particularly. No."

The landlady cocked her head.

Oh. Lou felt her face flush. "I never said that before. I can't believe I said that. That's a horrible thing to say. I'm sorry. No, of course I miss her. That's a horrible thing to say, right?" Lou felt a sick giggle erupting from her belly. She swallowed it back down.

"Maybe so, but I know what you mean. I feel that way about my own kid, for God's sake."

"Really? Dwayne's mother?" The giggle was rising now into Lou's shoulders. She could feel her lungs jumping without permission. She didn't get it. Nothing was funny.

"Really. My own child. She was wild. She just came out that way, I think, or I made her that way. Did herself in with drugs. How many times I found that baby of hers in a cold, wet diaper. No, I don't miss her. Junior's better off. No, that's not true. It's me. *I'm* better off."

The landlady looked Lou in the eye, and it was all over. She was laughing, too. Slowly, quietly, the way she did. Lou exhaled and let the laugh erupt. She took a swig of milk to rinse the words from her mouth. Her mouth was full of the unthinkable.

"I'm sorry. I'm sorry. We are terrible," Lou said.

"We are. We are terrible."

"I won't tell anybody," Lou said.

"Don't you dare," said the landlady.

. . .

Back upstairs at Lou's apartment, Julian was whining behind the door as she worked her key in the lock. He swished between her feet while she cracked open a can of fancy tuna. "I'm sorry to keep you waiting, buddy. I got to talking."

She left him to his dinner and settled sideways in the big chair to watch television, legs flopped over one fat armrest, back against the other. Julian came into the room licking his chops, then hunkered on her abdomen and purred. Lou thought of fat Gladys down in the basement, pushing her swollen gut against her cozy cage walls, getting ready to issue more needy beings. She thought of the way Julian used to hunker on Mother's abdomen, same as he did now, in the hospital bed they had installed in Mother's living room. Lou had to shoo the cat, over and over, off the skinny, sick belly in the bed. Until Mother shooed Lou away, too.

Go meet a man while you still have your figure.

Mother, I am not leaving you alone.
Why not? That's what I'll be doing to you.
Please, Mother. Don't talk like that.
Nobody else will. Somebody's got to.
Please, Mother.
Don't be naïve, Lou.

Lou had missed her then. Standing by the sickbed, with the woman right there at arm's length, Lou missed her. She wasn't even sure what she missed. Mother was still breathing, still bearing the unbearable.

She remembered the way Mother used to hold Julian, her fluffy baby, in the bend of her elbow, and carry him around like that, folding shirts and dusting sills and opening doors with her other hand, full of tender intention, before those arms gave up.

To be held. To be held like a treasure. Mother-arms: muscled, bones not yet brittle, fat still bewailed in moments of vanity. Skin not yet turned to rice paper, mind not yet stuck in a bitter circle. Lou missed this. She missed it, then wondered if she was imagining or remembering it. Can you miss the nonexistent? The never-was?

Don't be naïve.

Lou scratched Julian's neck, under his collar, the way he liked, the way Mother used to. He thanked Lou by poking his claws through her shirt into her belly fat. "Be nice." She did not shoo him off. She shook him by the scruff of the neck. His skin went taut over the bones of his pushed-in, pedigreed face, and his eyes looked surprised. His lips pulled back from his teeth in something like a smile. He went limp. He let go.

...

Surgery day arrived, and Gladys was no different: still

alone in her trap, purring, and beside herself with hunger. "No food today, sweeties," Lou said. "It will all be over soon."

Dwayne Junior rode along in the old, behemoth station wagon, fiddling with radio buttons until Lou put her hand on his to make him stop. In the back, not a word from the cats. Julian would be yowling bloody murder by now. Lou kept checking over her shoulder to make sure they were still there. Dwayne Junior, too, was quiet. He leaned his head on the window and watched the blocks go by.

Generators buzzed at the mobile clinic, parked outside a North Brooklyn shelter. Lou waited to fill out papers while Dwayne Junior brought cages from the car and stacked them at the curb. "Who's your helper?" said the cat lady ahead of Lou on line. Lou recognized her. She had a hairy overcoat and homemade hat and the air of someone who doesn't know when a conversation is over.

"My neighbor. He's been great."

"I have three kittens this time," said the lady. "I think they might become friendlies with just a little work. You?"

"Just the ferals. No friendlies. A couple young'uns." Lou tried to avoid the woman's eye as she hastily turned in her clipboard.

...

She and Dwayne Junior returned a few hours later for pickup. The chatty lady had found an audience in one of the techs, who had the exhausted smile of the habitually kind. Lou hoped to avoid further discussion, but another tech emerged from the vehicle and announced the results of her trapping: "You had six boys, four girls. One pregnant. Third trimester."

The chatty lady clapped her hands. "You caught a pregnant one! That's terrific!" She slapped Lou on the back. "Just in time!"

The tech didn't congratulate, just ran over his instruction sheet. "They're still a little jumpy from the drugs. I think you can let the boys go tonight if you want. Keep the girls another forty-eight hours, unless they get super restless. Except number—" He looked at the sheet. "Number seven."

"Gladys," Lou said.

"Yeah. She's had a rough day. She might need an extra day or so inside, if you can manage it."

"*Of course* we can manage it," Dwayne Junior said.

The tech locked eyes quizzically with Lou, and she nodded. "We can."

Dwayne Junior didn't say a word as they loaded the cages back into the station wagon. On the ride home, the cats mewed and banged their heads against the wire, waking up to their disfigurement: snipped ears to mark the occasion, glued incisions, important parts missing. Dwayne Junior, too, banged his head against the window. Lou stole glances, but traffic was difficult. The kid was in a state. "Want to find us something on the radio?" she said.

He shook his head.

"You sure? I liked that disco station you found before. Anything you want, though. Even sports. I don't listen to sports, but if you want."

He didn't look at her. He looked out the window. "What happened to her kittens?" he asked.

"They were euthanized." She could have lied, but she knew he wouldn't believe her.

"You mean killed."

"Yes, I mean killed."

"I could have taken care of them," he said.

"I know. You would have done good."

"I thought you loved animals. Gran said you're an animal lover."

"I am. I feel like I am. It's complicated."

He went back to banging his head against the window, scratching his temple occasionally. Lou feared he would dig a bloody patch.

"Will you still be able to help me take care of them in the basement? Just for two more days?"

"Will I *be able to*, or *do I want to*?"

"Do you want to?"

"I have to think about it."

"Okay."

From the back of the car came a thud and a whimper. One of the cats had tried, and failed, to stand up, still woozy from the anesthesia. Dwayne Junior didn't even turn to look.

. . .

He decided not to help her with the post-op care. The landlady was disappointed but didn't force him. Lou brought the boys to the graveyard that night, one by one, in their traps, and they scrambled from the cages into the shrubbery. She tended to the girls in silence, in the basement, alone, using the cafeteria-tray method Dwayne Junior had invented.

When the time came, she took the girls, all but one, and let them go, too. She bleached the cages in the basement sink and stacked them up against the wall. Dwayne Junior did not drop by. She went upstairs to bed.

Julian curled up on her belly, under the covers. She let him. She pet his head, slowly, and scratched under his collar, until she felt his purr go quiet. He was asleep.

She could not sleep. Each time she closed her eyes, she saw the same picture. It made her shoo Julian off and get up; it made her paw through the pantry for a can of milk; it made her put a coat over her pajamas and flip-flop down to the basement. A single, covered cage was adrift in the middle of the floor; inside it, Gladys, silent. Lou lifted back the sheet. Gladys hid in the rear of her trap. Her ear was scabbed where they had lopped off the tip. She was a different cat. She was not the cat who had lolled and rolled in the same cage, yearning for what was coming next, yearning to be yearned for. The cat did not move when Lou opened the hatch. She crouched and waited while Lou poured a small dish of milk. She waited for Lou to close the door. Then she stepped forward and drank.

A small gesture, and probably not enough. Lou stayed and sat and watched the cat drink. She did not go back upstairs to sleep. She knew the picture would come back; the picture would stick with her, the way sticky pictures do. It would sneak into a perfectly pleasant afternoon; it would undo all the good of her intentions, this thing she had imagined but never seen: a shiny sac in the palm of the tech at the mobile clinic, and a needle poking through the sac, through new orange fur, and wet skin, and ribs, into the throbbing light of the unwanted creature, into the throbbing light.

Captivity

Anthony Sorge

I THOUGHT ABOUT STUFFING THE FIRST DRAFT of this letter into the mailbox of your old house. The shed where we stole the bolt cutter is gone, though—just a sparse sheet of grass sprouting like Silas Crane's mustache from the darkened patch of yard where it had been—and there's a new car in the driveway. A Jeep with a FREEDOM ISN'T FREE bumper sticker on the back. Some hulking plastic toys in sun-bleached primary colors in the front yard. I wondered if the new people had any idea where you and your mom and her boyfriend went after the foreclosure, but I decided against going up to the door and asking. The letter didn't say everything it had to say yet anyway.

...

I think I was around seven when my mom started taking me to the petting zoo on her good days—the days when she would emerge from the bathroom like the beautiful twin sister of the woman with the matted hair and the red, itchy skin who, on most days, only came out of her bedroom to pee or eat some potato chips over the sink. Neither of us cared much about the zoo; it was just the closest kid-friendly location to the house. The day the doe arrived, the owner tied some half-inflated balloons to the ticket booth to welcome the new addition to the Bohuski Zoo Family. Some of the kids were shaking her fence, asking their parents why the doe wouldn't *do anything*, and some were even throwing pellets into the enclosure before growing impatient and turning their backs to her. The doe just stood there, not in frozen terror but with a dignified contempt for her surroundings. I looked away, vaguely ashamed, and rejoined my mom at the pigpen. I told her I wanted to leave.

That night, my eyes drifted from my homework to the window above my desk. In the early summer twilight, I thought I could see the spectral shapes of spindly legged deer in the backyard, the white of their tails flickering like candle flames as they wove in and out of the darkness of the woods. What was it that had made the other animals' captivity at the petting zoo seem so normal, so natural and mundane? Somehow, it had never occurred to me that a pig, a goat, or a chicken would live anywhere but a fenced-in enclosure on the side of the road. But the doe's presence there just felt wrong.

Eventually we stopped going to the zoo altogether. I got too old, and things with my mom got much worse. Either that, or I had just started to see things more clearly: By then, I had found out about the pills, the reason for the perpetually closed bedroom door, the source of the plastic rattling sound that had haunted my dreams when I was little. My mom's good days became more and more infrequent, and the bad days became worse: smashed plates and *Exorcist*-level curses at night and crying jags or amnesia in the morning. Except for school, I rarely left the house. There weren't any other kids in our neighborhood, just a couple of teenagers whose skateboards occasionally rumbled past our house on their way to the convenience store a couple of blocks away. I read a lot. I looked out the window a lot.

Then I met you.

You were new, and you walked through the halls with the same force field around you that I did—hood up, headphones on, hair draped over your eyes. Our friendship seemed to spring from that foundation, fully formed—an Athena of a friendship, fierce and armored.

We didn't have many classes together, but you sat next to me in art, and I'd get mesmerized watching you paint; I often found my attention wandering from my own lifeless still lifes to your giant canvases of dirty red and smudgy gray and glossy black, alien animals with haunted, hunted expressions, caged by emaciated trees. They reminded me of the doe, and that made me like you even more.

One afternoon, I ran back to the art room to get the bag I'd forgotten earlier in the day and found you hunched over your canvas, tinny music seeping out of your headphones. You asked me if I wanted to hang out and draw for a while. I had never missed the bus, never come home late. I knew there would be consequences. But I had also never been asked to "hang out" before. I pulled up a stool beside you, and you offered me one of your earbuds. I brought it to my ear, the thin, pinched music growing in resonance, and felt like you and I were sharing the same brain.

"Is your mom, like, really strict?" you asked me as you drove me home an hour or so later. And I wanted to tell you everything—about the injury that had gotten her the disability checks and her first taste of painkillers, about the closed bedroom door and the stink of her unwashed body when she'd plop onto the couch next to me to watch cartoons for a minute before dozing off, about staring out the window and wondering what the rest of the kids from my class were doing—the birthday parties, the soccer games, the bike rides—while I re-did the word searches in my ninety-nine-cent activity book, trying not to see the indentations of the pencil marks I'd erased. But I didn't tell you any of that; I just said, "Yeah, I guess."

You said your mom was cool, but her boyfriend was a dick, and the way you said it made me feel the same way I did when you offered me the earbud.

You dropped me off, after the convenience store and the coffee and the park with the broken swings and mushroom graffiti everywhere, and I wanted nothing more than to chase after you as you pulled away, to climb back into that little escape pod. But you were gone, and the windows were so fogged up I couldn't even see you inside the car as you rounded the corner.

I wandered into my house, unsure whether I'd just returned to or from an alien world. I was so out of it I forgot to say hi to my mom, who went on a rampage as soon as she saw me stumbling into the kitchen. She wanted to know why I was late and if I knew how hungry she was and if I was ever planning on making dinner, and I looked at her standing there, the glow of the laptop behind her shining through her threadbare pajamas, and the hatred snuck up on me. I'd never hated her before, at least not consciously, never hated the guilt trips and the tirades and the fear that kept me cooped up in that house for seventeen years. But that was before I knew you were out there, before I knew what she was holding me back from.

It was ugly, and I don't remember exactly what I said, only the stunned, dumb look on my mom's face while I was saying it. But just like how you know when you're done puking, I knew when I was done yelling, when I'd purged myself of all the resentment and disappointment and rage that had been festering inside me for so long, and when I was empty, we just stared at each other as if from across a huge crater like Goku and Cell in *Dragon Ball Z*, and because there was nothing else to do, I turned around and walked out.

I felt like I'd beaten a boss at the end of a level, like triumphant 8-bit music was going to start playing any second. A spell had been broken.

I didn't know where I was going, but I guess I wasn't totally surprised when I ended up at the petting zoo. It was closed for the day, but the gate hanging off its hinges wasn't a huge deterrent. I hadn't been there in years, and even though it seemed smaller than I remembered, everything else came rushing back to me: the smells of hay and dung and wool and animal breath, the sound of claws and beaks on metal and concrete, the brays and whines and grunts of longing. The goats trotted to their fence like dogs, nagging me for attention and treats, but I walked right past them to the maintenance shed, tiptoeing and slowing my pace on the wood-chip path without really knowing why. I had to remind myself to breathe; was she still there?

Where else would I be? she seemed to reply. She greeted me with the same stare she'd left me with. The leaves overhead dropped flecks of shadow on her like flower petals. And I guess it was then that I decided I'd get her out.

...

Normally, I made a beeline for the art room as soon as I walked into school in the morning, dodging the Hacky Sack circles and football bros running plays in the hallway, but mostly trying to avoid the attention of Silas Crane and his friends prowling the halls, looking for some wounded animal to pounce on. But you picked me up and drove me to school that morning, and I felt invincible, even when Silas and his crew rolled up on us, so close we could see the pizza grease oozing out of their pores and hear the Eminem songs on the earbuds dangling down the fronts of their hoodies. Silas called us dykes, and you spat in his face just as Mr. Andretti was rounding the corner, and we darted away, cackling like witches.

You suggested we take the rest of the day off to celebrate our victory over Silas, our narrow escape from Mr. Andretti's clutches. So we did.

I couldn't believe how easy it was to just walk out. I half expected a phalanx of security guards to descend on us before our feet hit the blacktop, but no one noticed. And when we left school grounds completely, I could barely keep myself from busting out giggling. We were free! And all around us, other free people! And even though some guy honked at us and shouted something gross through the tattered sheet of plastic duct-taped over his broken passenger-side window, I felt the same way I felt after the fight with my mom, like I'd stepped through a portal to another dimension.

...

The bolt cutter hung, like Macbeth's floating dagger, in the shed where your parents hid the spare house key. From the moment I saw the tool, I thought I could see the whole chain of events laid out in front of me. I was right about most of it, I guess.

Your house looked like one of those roadside shrines to car-accident victims: candles; cheap stuffed animals, the kind absent-minded guys buy at convenience stores on the way home from work on Valentine's Day; and pictures in gaudy frames—Jesus, the Virgin Mary (even a holographic picture where Mary's placid face twisted into agony when you walked by), and a family in happier times: your mom, short and squat and looking older than she was, but smiling; your mom's ogre of a boyfriend with his meaty, hairy arm draped around her and pressed into the soft fat of her neck; and a little girl in between them, her face contorted into one of those violent, fake smiles little kids use in all their pictures. In some of the pictures, the girl was older, posed in front of the marbled backgrounds that characterized all school photos, awkward and chubby and sulky in black T-shirts emblazoned with the inscrutable logos of metal bands, her left eye peering out from behind her bangs, all but swallowed by a black hole of eyeliner.

We listened to music in your room until we got bored, and I suggested we go to the zoo. "There's someone I want you to meet," I said coyly, and you threw a pillow at me and called me a weirdo but said okay.

. . .

"Whoa," you said when you saw the doe. "She looks *pissed*."

Your reaction wasn't as eloquent as I would have hoped, but I could hear the awe in your voice, and I felt proud, like I had pleased her by bringing her another admirer, another person who really *saw* her, her beauty and her defiance, and not just another cute animal to gape at through a film of boredom. And even though I wouldn't mention the plan to you until later that night, I felt proud that we were going to get her out of there.

. . .

I sat in your bedroom the next night, listening to the sound of plates rattling with every slammed fist on the kitchen counter, your mom's boyfriend's voice booming through the floorboards and mingling with the music you'd put on before he bellowed for you to come downstairs. A few minutes later you burst into the room, all fists and gritted teeth and gulps for air. I grabbed you by the shoulders and pushed your bangs out of your eyes, the color of storm clouds, the levees of your eyeliner breaching and spilling muddy tears down your cheeks. I didn't ask what was wrong, and you didn't tell me, but I thought I could feel it, passing like static shocks through the tiny space between us as we sat next to each other on the floor—the same way I felt it across the doe's fence at the zoo. But I didn't know. And I didn't ask.

"We'll free the doe," I whispered as you dozed off. "And then we're next."

...

The black hoodie you loaned me was an enchanted cloak, bleeding into the blackness of the night. You trailed behind me, your pale face like a hole cut in a sheet of black construction paper before the motion sensor caught us and splashed us with light. We hopped the fence and crouched low as we ran behind the ticket booth, out of sight of the street.

The animals knew something was up. They emerged sleepily from their little sheds, taking confused steps to their fences and peering at us through the mesh. In the near darkness, even the sheep looked a little spooky, draped in their moon-colored wool. We leaned against the ticket booth and caught our breath before running to the maintenance shed in front of the doe's enclosure.

She looked like she'd been waiting for us, like she'd been standing in that same spot since the time I brought you to see her. I greeted her in a whisper and told her that she was going to be free.

The chain clanked on the metal gate as you brought the mouth of the bolt cutter to one of its thick links, and the uproar began. The chickens began fluttering their useless wings and rattling their fences, clucking like people speaking in tongues on the TV church shows. The goats launched into a dissonant chorus of monotone *bahh*s, their moist dog-noses pressed into the mesh of their fences, and the pig started running up and down the length of his enclosure, snorting and huffing and squealing anxiously. The din grew with every rattle of the chain, and I tried to hush the animals as best I could, *shhh*ing them and kicking pebbles into their enclosures while you grunted over the rusty bolt cutter, gnawing a groove into the chain link.

I hadn't expected it to be this hard. We'd even practiced in the shed behind your house, snipping a little chain we'd laid on the ground without too much trouble. But this chain was about twice as thick and at shoulder level, so we couldn't rest the bolt cutter against the ground and lean our weight into it as we had when we'd practiced. I was getting frustrated; a car swooshed by, and I ducked, feeling less confident in the protective powers of your hoodie. I watched the bolt cutter shake as your arms shivered and twitched from cold, anxiety, and weakness in the shaft of harsh light falling from the corner of the maintenance shed. For the first time, it occurred to me that maybe we wouldn't be able to get the doe out after all.

The thought sent me into a frenzy. I pushed you out of the way and took the bolt cutter myself, my veins bulging with adrenaline. You leaned against the maintenance shed and tried to catch your breath. For all your effort, you'd only carved a rough furrow about halfway through the chain link, but with one bite, I sent the two steel halves clattering to the ground.

"You did it!" you gasped, but I barely heard you and didn't reply. I was tugging at the chain, unwinding its seemingly endless length from around the gate until I tossed it to the ground like a dead snake and swung the gate open, its metal screeching in protest as it scraped against the concrete.

"You're free," I whispered.

The doe didn't seem to realize it, though. She just stood there, as still as the first time I'd visited her as a little girl and every time after, her gaze cast straight ahead. I crept into the enclosure, and even then she didn't flinch. It wasn't until I brought my hand to her neck, gently stroking the bristly fur, that she seemed to acknowledge me. She swung her eyes in a slow arc to meet mine, and my gaze fell to the ground, involuntarily.

"I don't think she wants to go." Your words tiptoed into the enclosure, and you followed.

"She's just weirded out," I said. "She doesn't know what to do." I gave her a shove, hoping to trigger some kind of muscle memory, an all-but-forgotten instinct for bounding through thickets and copses and labyrinthine forests. She stumbled a little and swung her eyes back to mine. The haughty defiance I'd seen from across the fence was gone, replaced with confusion and frustration and a dumb kind of pain.

"Maybe we should leave her here," you said.

"We just need to coax her a little." I gave her another shove, and her hooves clattered on the cement as she regained her balance. Again, that pathetic look in her eyes. It made me angry. Another shove, harder this time. She snorted a little, fidgeted.

You put your hand on my arm. "I think maybe we should try to close the gate back up."

And I guess that's where it gets blurry.

I don't remember pushing you, but I remember seeing you looking up at me from the ground, scared. You said I was freaking you out. And I remember shoving the doe, again and again, her hooves dragging on the concrete as I pushed her through the open gate. I remember how she swung her head back to look at me, and how you looked at me the same way but didn't try to stop me.

And as she made her way past the chickens and the goats and the pig and past the ticket booth, I remember thinking that I'd done it. That I'd saved her. That even if she was scared, the life she was walking into was a million times better than another second of captivity and humiliation. I had to believe that. If I didn't, what would it mean for us?

Then I heard you screaming. I saw you running to catch the doe, who'd almost made it to the road, and I remember the way the headlights swung around the corner like lasers ricocheting off a mirror. And I remember the sound, the agonizing screech punctuated by the *thud* I felt in my guts, and I remember seeing the car doors swing open, and the guys in the white baseball caps running out to examine their front bumper, and you sprinting into the road and falling to your knees in front of the doe, whose body was still facing in the direction of the stand of trees across the street, but whose neck had swung backwards unnaturally so her eyes could find mine.

And I remember running. Not toward you and the car and the doe but the other way, through woods that swirled around me like the whirlpools of black and black-green and black-brown in your paintings, my sneakers soaked with the muck of a shallow brook that slithered across my path, your hoodie slashed with briars and jagged tree limbs, the roar of crickets and frogs and leaf-crunch flooding my ears until I emerged into a cul-de-sac, a ring of motion-sensor lights flicking on around me like eyeballs snapping open. I slunk along a line of hedges, trying to orient myself and stay out of sight, looking for familiar houses or landmarks and finding none. The street spilled into another, and that into another, and I staggered under the streetlights as the stars retreated with the sun's slow march over the horizon until my house materialized in front of me.

I woke up the next morning with my bed full of prickers. They needled me as I rolled over to pull the blind over my window, as if to preempt any confusion about whether what had happened the night before had been a dream. I thought about calling you but didn't. Couldn't.

My mom's bedroom door was closed. I told her she needed to call me in sick and she yelled something back, muffled by the comforter pulled over her head and the door between us.

I brushed most of the prickers out of my bed and crawled back in.

You weren't in school the next day, and I kind of hoped that would be it—that you'd just disappear so I'd never have to face you. We managed to steer clear of each other for the rest of senior year, and the day after graduation, I found a room to rent in the city on Craigslist and didn't look back.

. . .

The phone call from the hospital dragged me back, though. My mom. They were sorry to inform me, etc. I did an okay job of sounding sad on the phone, but I felt like they were telling me I'd won a sweepstakes I'd entered years ago and had completely given up on. The prize had looked like freedom once, but it hadn't aged well.

I crossed the expanse of highway in an under-caffeinated daze; static enshrouded the NPR reporters without my noticing and then released them some time later to repeat the cycle of headlines and field reports, making me feel like I hadn't moved at all. I signed some papers and made some arrangements, saving the hard work for another trip.

Before I left, I made the loop around town, the tour of our short history together: the high school, your house, my house, all shrunk by time but still retaining their psychic energy, the kind that make the EVP recorders and EMF readers light up on those paranormal investigator shows. And then the last stop—the one that pulled me away from the highway on-ramp and got me to finish this letter.

Like everything else in town, the petting zoo had gotten smaller; a shopping plaza had emerged next door, or at least the shell of one, and its parking lot had swallowed half of the pig's enclosure and pushed the ticket booth up against the goats' fence. The woods at the far end—the woods I had run through that night, that had rolled me around in their mouth and spit me out—seemed to have encroached on the zoo, too, their dark green limbs hovering possessively overhead. A chain hung loosely around the entrance gate, but I slipped inside easily and without thinking, making my way to the maintenance shed—slouching and shedding paint chips on the grass below—as if pulled by a tractor beam.

Behind it, the fence still stood, enclosing the slab of concrete that had cracked into chunks like an ice floe, thick shocks of wispy, tick-ridden grass and foxtails and milkweed filling the fissures. The placard, full of "fun facts" and a little biography of the doe, dangled from a zip tie and was covered with Sharpie graffiti and bird shit. I'd never bothered to read it.

A BLIND DEER DOESN'T STAND MUCH OF A CHANCE IN THE WILD, it read.

I moaned and dropped the placard. One of the sheep replied, but otherwise, the zoo was silent.

I turned to leave and locked eyes with the chicken. She was standing on the ramp of her coop, watching me, cocking her head to one side and then another, a quiet stream of clucks rolling out of her throat like the sound of a pot of pasta on a low boil. I read the placard on her fence; the names of the other chickens had been painted over, making her Willa. I whispered hello, and she took a couple of uncertain steps down the ramp.

I resisted the idea as soon as I noticed it creeping into my head. Yeah, there was garbage everywhere, and she was all alone, and she'd have to endure days and days and days of kids yelling and poking and prodding and tossing pellets at her before the zoo owner would find her dead in her coop. I felt cursed: How could I be sure that a life outside of the cage would be any better than this?

I said good-bye to Willa. Her clucks rose in volume a little, but she didn't seem terribly disappointed; how many backs had turned to her in her life? But as I sat in my car, looking at the faded sign hanging above the ticket booth, I thought of you. I thought of how maybe I couldn't have saved you from your mom's boyfriend and the jerks at school, how maybe we never could have gotten free, but I could have made it suck a little less. I could have been a friend.

There was a box in my trunk, full of old CDs I was going to trade in at Disc N DAT for some extra cash. I dumped them out and lined the box with a cast-off hoodie from the back seat. I pulled my keys out of the ignition and punched holes in the box. And then I went back for Willa.

Since I can't go back for you, I guess that's the best I can do.

The Truth of Ten Thousand Things

Hunter Liguore

SANCHE DIDN'T WANT TO GO and see the bear die. "Too sad, Ponytail. Too sad."

"It's a big moment," Yunnan explained over the phone. "Lots of families are going together. Big stars are coming from Hollywood. Cave Bear will be there. We always loved her."

"No, Ponytail, too sad. But Papi will be there."

In the past, whenever Yunnan got news of her papi being somewhere, she didn't go. Like the time Sanche sang in the World Peace Chorus at Rockefeller Center. She'd watched it on the TV and told her sister that she was the loudest singer. Or last year when Sanche gave a workshop at the public library on tea ceremonies. Or last month when Sanche's daughter, Lucy, turned ten and relatives she'd never seen before arrived in New York from Guangxi.

"But he can't go, Sanche. I'm going. Can you tell him?" She felt a juvenile impulse swell up in her, despite being forty-five. She wanted to tell Sanche that she called it first. Papi had no right showing up.

"You know Papi. No one can change his mind once it's made."

"Yeah," said Yunnan quietly. "I know."

. . .

It was time to put the white bear to rest. Yunnan had been following Betty's story for the past two years in *The New Yorker*. Betty was named after the actress Betty Dandy, who died the same year the bear was taken out of the wild and put into the zoo. The actress had lived to be a hundred and twelve, and animal activists thought if the white bear could live just as long then there might be a chance science could put things right.

But here it was two years later, and Betty was emaciated and ghostly, with black eyes that looked like potholes. Cancer will do that from the inside. A stomach full of plastic didn't help either. Of course, Yunnan, along with the rest of the world, rooted for Betty's survival. She hosted a weekly blog detailing the events of Betty's life, how much fish she ate, when she swam, which celebrity donated money for genetic research. But as Betty's vitality dwindled, Yunnan's posts took on a more desperate tone. *Betty needs our help. Betty can't do it without us. Betty is our last hope.*

But few commented on Yunnan's posts. Instead they were on to the new fad science created, a temporary solution to extinction—the polar puff smart-bear™. Using the best parts of Betty's genes, the scientists at NoEndanger Labs created a miniature version of Betty. Polar puffs were the same size as a pet rabbit, with fur as soft as a synthetic Russ toy. And it was believed that they could talk, although when Yunnan took her five-year-old son, Jinhai, to the pet shop, she couldn't make out what the little puff was uttering.

Ho-ho-ho chi burp. Ho-ho-ho chi burp. Ho-ho-ho chi burp.

"It said hello, Momi. Did you hear it?" Jinhai pressed his face to the metal cage, his tiny index finger wiggling to touch the bear's fur.

She bought one, took it home, and watched it die two days later. Workers from the pet shop came and bagged the polar puff, which had turned a bright, splotchy red from all the blood that had blossomed to the surface.

"Did I kill it?" Jinhai's face was red from crying.

"No one killed it. It just died." In her mind she heard her papi's voice. She was transported to her childhood home, the one her parents still lived in. A starling had collided with the mini-windmill on the roof and broke its neck. Yunnan picked it up, straightened the beak, and petted the iridescent feathers. "Papi, why do things die?"

"To force us to march straight into fear and suffering."

"Did the bird suffer?"

"No, only you are experiencing suffering, Yunnan, because you cannot see that in the moment the bird died it was given freedom from life and reborn. See?" Papi pointed to a starling perched in the tree. Yunnan placed the dead bird in the grass, and weightlessly ran toward the tree, calling to the bird. For many years she'd believed the dead bird had become the one in the tree.

...

Yunnan and Jinhai wore matching Betty shirts to the "Good-bye, Betty" send-off at the Bronx Zoo. Lots of money had been raised on tickets and merchandise to support scientists who promised to prevent other animals from extinction.

"We couldn't help Betty," said the NoEndanger Lab spokesperson during the opening ceremony, "but we can help many other species. With your donations and support, we won't ever have to have another good-bye send-off."

Yunnan treated Jinhai to a vegan patty shaped like the cartoon version of Betty on the Nic-All-Day Network. She bought him an eco-balloon that turned into oatmeal when it popped. Together they took a ride through an interactive tunnel that gave the history of polar bears, explaining that Betty's fate was inevitable; early guesses blamed global warming or increased drilling when the ice melted, but all arrows pointed to the fact that all species die out eventually.

In the afternoon, they listened to a kid-aged lecture on ways to help other creatures like Betty. Yunnan had heard most of it before. The message used to be: Get informed, get accountable, and get busy changing the way you live. Now it was: Support science, support a critter who needs it, and support our new world.

A crowd gathered at the back of the room. Cave Bear had arrived. In the crowd Yunnan looked for her papi. She wondered if she'd recognize him, if he'd still have the same hollow eyes and cement chin with lips that stretched in an empty straight line.

Yunnan took Jinhai by the hand and led him toward the Arctic Trail. Thick lines of people stretched like tentacles from the white tunnels that led to Betty's icy home at the center.

Jinhai tugged on her wrist. "That man's staring."

Papi stood taller than the rest, or so it felt to Yunnan, who had put him on a high shelf, out of reach and out of sight. He could've been smiling, but all she saw was disapproval.

It started twelve years ago when she decided to have a child on her own. Papi was still talking to her then, though it was fragmented, the way a haiku poem is, and often with a similarly cryptic message.

Women not have child
 Alone
Family of two
Heartache will follow

Unconventional
Yunnan knows best
 Big mistake
She will never learn

She thought Papi would relent when the baby came, but instead she received silence, a permanent rapture to a place far from reconciliation. She tried for the first year to bait him with pictures and cards signed in her handwriting with love from Jinhai. But he believed science shouldn't make a baby. Or was it that a child should be raised with two parents? Yunnan had given up trying to guess what Papi was thinking. In the mornings when she sat *zazen*, she saw his unyielding face, past and present, never-changing—always there keeping her from centering on the quiet present.

And now there he was, a stranger among a crowd of other strangers. She kept his stare.

Yunnan knew the division between them had been there as far back as when she was a teenager, brave and fearless, a girl who didn't need her papi's philosophy on how to live her life.

Whoever knows does not speak. Whoever speaks does not know.

She fought him in every decision. If he said college, she said travel. If he said sit *zazen*, she said standing tai chi. In her twenties she did eventually go to college to become a teacher of Chinese literature, making clear to him that it was her decision, not his wish, that prompted her. Sanche stayed neutral through all of it, as did her mother, who said, "You always push him and leave him no place to dwell in your life."

Yunnan didn't want to hear it. She saw in Papi what they couldn't see—a jealous old man who didn't like to see his daughter outdo him, especially on her own merits.

A cloud of anger clenched at her body, making it tight and strained. Yunnan turned back to the line, now moving. She concentrated on her breath. *Breathe in. Feel the cool air on the back of the throat. Center. Breathe out.* She did this five times, then lost her drive toward ten, seeing only Papi behind her eyes. She looked back in the crowd, thinking maybe she'd say something like, *Go away.* But Papi was gone. She wondered then if she'd seen him at all.

...

At the end of the Arctic Trail, Yunnan and Jinhai sat on the blue recycled-materials bleachers in the arena, facing Betty's habitat, an artificial ice island with a cutout cave and circular pool. Several gen-mod seals did tricks in the pool while the trainer explained that the new breed of seals no longer needed ice, which increased their overall chance of survival.

Next up to entertain the crowd were the grolar bears—half grizzly, half polar—and they looked more like big cows to Yunnan.

"When will we see Betty?" Jinhai's eyes grew sleepy.

Yunnan tucked him close, allowing him to rest his head in her lap. "Soon. I promise." She no longer watched the bear tricks but scanned the rows of faces, most expressing joy at watching the show. Papi wasn't anywhere she could see, allowing her to drop her shoulders and just be.

She started to focus on her breathing again, a technique she'd modified since learning it from Papi as a child. But no matter how she tried, she couldn't shake him from her thoughts. She was about to give up when a memory cascaded into her thoughts.

Papi had taken her and Sanche to their uncle's farm near the Connecticut border. Yunnan was fifteen at the time. Uncle Tato was experimenting with raising rice paddies and had asked Papi for advice. Yunnan had lingered behind them, across the field indented with mud squares filled with goop. Uncle Tato called her over. "See, if we can grow rice here, we can feed so many people. These rice plants will yield one hundred and fifty pounds of hearty rice. That's one paddy. And look, see, there are a dozen."

Uncle Tato was so excited, youthful, and undeterred. But rather than share in the excitement, Papi tore at Tato's vision, saying it was a waste of time and energy.

Yunnan remembered the sad look in Uncle Tato's eyes, sad like the dead starling, as if all his vital force had been sucked out of him. At that moment she and Tato shared something. Without giving it much thought, she took Tato's arm and said, "I want to help. Show me what I can do." Uncle Tato came back a little, his spirit reincarnating a step at a time, until he was knee-high in mud, showing her how to aerate the paddy. Behind them Papi scowled.

Yunnan came back to the present when the audience clapped. She clapped along, smiling when Jinhai looked up at her. She had missed a moment. All her learning about the right way of living said *be present*. Don't allow the future that hasn't happened strangle you, nor allow the past that has already happened possess you. Instead, appreciate the moment as it unfolds. It was all she had. But her estrangement with Papi was keeping her in the past, in the unhappy place of *what if.*

She focused her breathing, raising her eyes to the platform that ascended from the fake ice. On it, lying sideways on a bed of straw, was Betty. The local high school band played a song as people stood, cheering. Yunnan lifted Jinhai to her hip so he could see. "You will remember this your whole life, Jinhai. You can say you saw the last polar bear die."

Through the crowd, a figure moved toward her. At first she saw Papi's face; then she saw the reality of what was in front of her. It was Sanche and Lucy.

They hugged as Sanche asked what she missed.

"It's just getting started."

Sanche sat next to Yunnan while Lucy sat with Jinhai, who showed off his balloon.

"Why did you come?"

"I realized I was trying to get even with you for not coming to Lucy's birthday," said Sanche, taking her sister's hand. "This morning after *zazen* I came upon a flower that had started to wilt. Small and frail, and yet very beautiful. I remembered that time is being lost, and nothing is permanent."

Yunnan understood. Through the knowledge that all things are temporary, the present was all the more appreciated.

Sanche pulled her sister closer, reminiscing. "Do you remember when we were little girls, probably no more than Jinhai's age, Papi took us to the circus?"

"We were much older."

"Oh, no, you were so tiny. Papi had wanted us to see an elephant. Do you remember?"

Yunnan tried to recall, but only a partial memory of a carnival glimpsed her thoughts.

"The elephant was just a baby, but to us it was enormous. We watched the acrobats do all sorts of tricks with it. We were picked out of the crowd to go up to it and feed it a peanut." Sanche started to laugh. "But when you got up close, it raised its trunk, and you started to cry. Papi came and took you outside."

"You're making this up."

"Don't you recall? On the way home I tied your hair into

a ponytail, like the elephant trunk, and we made noises until Papi yelled at us to stop. That's when I started calling you Ponytail."

"No, Sanche. It was when we were at Auntie Jinger's and she wanted to braid my hair, but you told her I liked ponytails, and since then she started calling me Ponytail Girl."

"Maybe you were too young to remember the elephant." Sanche didn't fight her. "You could ask Papi."

"I'll ask Momi."

"She didn't go with us. She went with Auntie Jinger to see *Tourandot*."

Yunnan was quiet. She felt a stabbing pain in her head, amplified by the clapping, the band music, and the cool air blowing off the ice pond. She didn't like feeling she didn't know something. It made her vulnerable.

"I'm glad you came," she said finally.

"Me, too."

. . .

Yunnan and Sanche agreed that Cave Bear would be the name they gave to their favorite American actress, Hannah Richmond, when she won a lifetime achievement award around the time Lucy was born. Cave Bear had become like the character in her first movie role—cast out by her own tribe but later ensuring its survival.

Without Cave Bear, the world would still be getting their food shipped from around the world. Thanks to the actress's leadership efforts, state-owned and -operated gardens sprouted up in major cities, spreading like a pandemic, offering a ready supply of food to each town's constituents. Soon came the vertical gardens, like the one near the Empire State Building, where Cave Bear held a hunger strike with half the residents of Manhattan. Her message was simple: We need to eat. Popularity won. Gardens were built. And slowly change occurred.

Now, here was their childhood idol, an older woman, still sleek, her hair no longer a crown of sunshine but a tender field of gray. Cave Bear had fought hard for Betty to remain in the wild.

Yunnan squeezed Sanche's hand, as if they were watching a sad scene in a movie. Cave Bear spoke a few words to the crowd, mostly reminding everyone that Betty was one of many endangered animals. "Science is intentionally trying to make people feel the situation is hopeless. It is *never* hopeless, unless you give up."

Yunnan stood, clapping. Jinhai took it as an opportunity to scream. Lucy joined him, and soon Sanche quieted them both.

The hour had come. Cave Bear knelt beside Betty, who had hardly moved, her cold eyes staring out. The doctors came out with a metal tray and two injections. Cave Bear was asked to give the first one. But she said she wouldn't, agreeing only to be there for Betty. She wrapped her arms around the thin shoulders, pressing her face into the yellowed fur. The crowd turned to ice, and all movement suspended.

...

The last time Yunnan spoke to Papi, they were sitting on the porch that looked out onto an urban street. They had argued for the better part of an hour about the struggles of raising a child alone, about the unnatural method of insemination, each accusing the other of having to be right in every situation. As the cars zoomed past, creating a border of noise, Yunnan heard her father slow his breathing. She recognized that he was attempting to ground himself. She wanted to do the same but didn't, not wanting him to think she was copying him. After a while, Papi spoke.

"Did I ever tell you about your Uncle Tato's sheep?"

"No." Her voice sounded defensive, despite his being tender. "I didn't know he had any sheep."

"It was a long time ago. One of the sheep got out of its pen and went into the woods. Tato went to look for it but realized that there was far too much ground to cover by himself, so he called all his workers together, and they split into groups. It was nightfall before everyone returned back to the farm. No one had found the sheep. Tato grew angry, calling his workers lazy, and accused them of going into the woods to sleep rather than look for the sheep. But one of his workers came forward and said, 'No, Tato, we tried our best to find the sheep, but no matter what path we took, we always came to a fork. We didn't know where to go or where to turn, or even how to get back to the farm.' Tato didn't want to believe him, but many of his workers said the same thing, that the forks in the road kept them from finding the sheep."

"Did he ever find out what happened to it?"

Papi didn't answer her. The sun grew dim overhead, and shadows pervaded the porch. Yunnan left and never returned. Oh, she had her moments of weakness—times when she saw a movie that made her homesick, or when Sanche related how Lucy had such a good time with her grandpi, fueling a snarl of jealousy.

Watching Betty's life release transported Yunnan back to the starling, up and down every road that led her to the porch, and all the forks that winded and twisted every which way, causing her to become the sheep, lost and forgetful of the way home.

The doctor pumped Betty with the second dose. A stranger's hand took hers from the left, and Yunnan held onto Sanche's with the right. Together, the audience formed a connected web of people, each praying, some singing or meditating; others, like Yunnan, were crying.

Somewhere in the audience was Papi. She looked for him, wanting to go to him, as if after all the years of fighting against him, she had finally let go.

Then a great, painful cry broke the unity.

Ho-ho-ho chi-burp. Ho-ho-ho chi burp.

"The polar bear said good-bye, Momi," said Jinhai. "Did you hear it?"

Betty seized and stilled.

"It's over," she said, hugging her son. Betty's struggle had ended. Like the starling, the bear would follow the cycle of death, back to life, through rebirth. It was as her papi taught her—*The Tao gives birth to the one, the one to the two, the two to the three; from the three are born the ten thousand things. The ten thousand things balance yin and yang, united in the primordial breath to bring about harmony.*

Cave Bear gave a nod to the doctors, wiping her eyes, standing, covering her face as cameras fought to get the exclusive. The crowd was complacent only for a few minutes, until a trainer announced a special 3-D movie of Betty's cartoon look-alike in the North Pole Center, and an exclusive chance to win the latest version of the polar puff smart-bear™.

"Will you stay with Jinhai?" she asked Sanche.

"Where are you going, Ponytail?"

Yunnan had already cut through the bleachers, on her way through the crowded tunnels, where the lines broke off in different directions. She lingered by a penguin signpost, searching for Papi. When she didn't find him, she changed sides and stood on a chair, the faces of the people expressing: *What is this crazy lady doing?*

The moment passed. The doubt rushed back in. Yunnan sat in the chair, shoulders slumped. When she glanced up,

Papi was standing over her. She was surprised to see him—not as in her memory, tough and durable, but aged and tired, frail like Betty.

She knew she only had the moment. "Papi," she cried, wrapping her arms around his neck, pressing her face into his shoulder, breathing in the familiar smell of childhood found in his shirt.

"You are no longer lost, little sheep?"

Yunnan felt her temper flare. It wasn't his words but merely his voice, the voice of a hundred moments across time when she'd always challenged him. She took a deep breath, smiling. "I am no longer lost," she said, remembering something she'd learned from her Zen teacher: The path is the goal. All her pushing Papi away, all her desire to show him she could take care of herself led to the moment of letting go. But as much as she wanted to stay in the present, she needed to rectify the past. "Why did you stop talking to me?"

"Why did you stop needing me?"

They were almost the same, but different. Yunnan wanted to say more; she wanted to resume the old shell of who she'd been with Papi, to fight him and say something clever. But the feeling subsided. Around her, kids paraded with stuffed polar bears. Time was fleeting. Her papi would pass on soon. All the time she'd wasted, she couldn't regain.

"Tomorrow can I see you? Will you let me bring Jinhai over to meet you?"

"Tomorrow? Years go by, and just like that you want to have your papi back in your life? Maybe you need to give this much thought. Maybe sit *zazen* and see where it leads you."

She didn't back down. "I have sat *zazen* every day—well, almost every day—for all these years, and the message is the same."

"Then why did you wait so long?"

The flow of people broke up their isolation, forcing them

to drift apart. Sanche was there with Lucy, who greeted her grandpi. Jinhai sleepily leaned into Yunnan. Not realizing that they were talking, Sanche treated them as she always had, divided, and pulled Papi along, waving good-bye to Yunnan.

This moment was passing. They would drift apart and maybe be taken down another thousand roads before finding one another again. That was the lesson of the ten thousand things. Only in forgetting the self could she be united with all things. All things. Papi.

"Papi." Her voice wasn't loud enough over the crowd. "Papi," she called again, lifting Jinhai to her waist. "Papi," she called, her sister's head moving out of view, until she couldn't see them anymore.

Then, with a terrible cry, Jinhai let rip, *"Ho-ho-ho chi-burp! Ho-ho-ho chi burp!"*

The crowd around them seemed to suspend, causing a gap straight to Papi. He turned, facing Yunnan, meeting eyes with Jinhai.

"Good-bye," howled Jinhai, waving.

Papi's always-straight lips curled. He lifted his hand and waved.

"You see that tall man, Jinhai? That is your grandpi." She wondered if Jinhai would remember, or if his memory would distort over time, like her own. "You can say you saw your grandpi for the first time here." She wanted to tell him that he'd get to meet grandpi tomorrow, but her way of life taught her that tomorrow was not a guarantee. What they had was now, and that, too, was fleeting.

As they followed the line of people out to the parking lot, Yunnan noticed the sky had turned crimson as the sun started its descent. She looked again, noticing that everywhere her eyes fell, things were a little brighter, a little less mysterious, a little bit reflective of the happiness in her heart.

Contributors

J. Bowers is a fiction writer whose work has appeared in *The Indiana Review, StoryQuarterly, The Portland Review*, and other national journals. She holds a Ph.D. in English from the University of Missouri and is currently a full-time faculty member in English at Maryville University, St. Louis.

Ramola D's first short fiction collection, *Temporary Lives*, was awarded the 2008 AWP Grace Paley Prize in Short Fiction and was a finalist in the 2010 Library of Virginia Fiction awards. Also a poet, teacher, and human-rights activist, she is the recipient of a 2005 NEA fellowship in poetry.

Anne Elliott is the author of *The Beginning of the End of the Beginning*, released by Ploughshares Solos in 2014. Her stories can be seen in *Crab Orchard Review, Witness, Hobart, Bellevue Literary Review, Fugue, r.kv.r.y*, and others. She lives in Portland, Maine, and is at work on a novel.

Catherine Evleshin grew up on a farm in California, then left the rural life for academe and the performing arts. Her stories appear in *Agave Magazine, Canary Journal of Environmental*

Crisis, Gemini Literary Magazine, Fiction Vortex, and *Riding Light Review*, among other publications.

Nels Hanson grew up on a small farm in the San Joaquin Valley of California and has worked as a farmer, teacher, and contract writer/editor. His fiction received the San Francisco Foundation's James D. Phelan Award and Pushcart nominations in 2010, 2012, and 2014. Poems appeared in *Word Riot, Oklahoma Review, Pacific Review*, and other magazines and received a 2014 Pushcart nomination, *Sharkpack Review*'s 2014 Prospero Prize, and 2015 and 2016 Best of the Net nominations.

JoeAnn Hart is the author of the novels *Float*, a dark comedy about plastics in the ocean, and *Addled*, a social satire about Canada geese at a country club. Her short fiction, essays, and articles have been widely published, including in *Orion* magazine and *Terrain.org*.

Claire Ibarra is in the MFA creative writing program at Florida International University. Her fiction has appeared in many fine literary journals and anthologies, including *Natural Bridge, Amoskeag, The MacGuffin*, and *Torched Anthology*. Claire has worked for nonprofits, teaching creative writing to incarcerated women in Florida. In addition to writing fiction, she enjoys poetry and photography.

Rachel King received a BA from the University of Oregon and an MFA from West Virginia University. Her fiction has appeared in *Concho River Review*, the *Farallon Review*, and in the *Museum of Americana*. Her poems have appeared in the *Blue Collar Review*, the *Aurorean, Windover*, and the *Penwood Review*. She lives in Portland, Oregon.

Hunter Liguore is an American writer with degrees in history and writing. She was named the 2015 Writer-in-Residence at the Edwin Way Tale Nature Preserve. A two-time Pushcart-Prize nominee, her work has appeared in various publications internationally. She teaches undergraduate and graduate writing in New England. Her forthcoming novel is represented by Regal Hoffman and Associates. www.HunterLiguore.com

C.S. Malerich lives and works near the District of Columbia. Her speculative fiction has appeared previously in *Ares Magazine, The Again*, and the first volume of *Among Animals*. She is a founding member of the collective DC Stampede, supporting grassroots organizing on behalf of animals, people, and the planet.

Carmen Marcus lives and writes in the British Victorian Spa town of Saltburn-by-the-Sea. As the daughter of an Irish mother and Yorkshire fisherman, her writing pulls together the magical and the practical. She has won numerous awards for poetry and fiction, including BBC Radio 3's New Voice 2015.

Sascha Morrell reads, writes, teaches, and scrambles over rocks on the Northern Tablelands of New South Wales, Australia. She completed her doctoral studies at the University of Cambridge before taking up a post as Lecturer in English at the University of New England (Australia) in 2013. She has published short fiction and poetry in numerous British and Australian literary journals. Her latest creative work explores the relationship between human beings and moths.

Robyn Ryle started life in one small town in Kentucky and ended up in another just down the river in southern

Indiana. Her chapbook, *The Face of Baseball*, is available from WhiskeyPaper Press. She has stories and essays in *CALYX Journal, Midwestern Gothic, Big Truths/Little Fiction*, and *Bartleby Snopes*, among others.

Anthony Sorge is a high school teacher, writer, and cartoonist from Connecticut. In addition to writing short fiction, Anthony has self-published the comic zine *Crust Dog* since 2011 and produces the podcast Another World.

Laura Maylene Walter is the author of *Living Arrangements* (BkMk Press). Her writing has appeared or is forthcoming in the *Kenyon Review, The Sun, Poets & Writers, Michigan Quarterly Review,* and elsewhere. She was a Tin House Scholar and a past fiction editor of *Mid-American Review.* She lives in Cleveland.

Acknowledgments

"It Won't Be Long Now" was originally published on eco-fiction.com in September of 2014. It was anthologized in *Winds of Change: Stories about Our Climate* (Moon Willow Press, 2015).

"Bight, Tomcat, and the Moon" was first published online on Word Factory in November of 2015.

"Lost Pets" first appeared in the Spring 2016 issue of *The South Carolina Review*.

"Vivarium" first appeared in *Sliver of Stone* magazine in April of 2014.

"A Normal Rabbit" first appeared in the Spring 2016 issue of *Concho River Review*.

"A Sterile Place" appeared in *Animal Literary Magazine* in May of 2013 and in *Ginosko Literary Journal* in 2014.

"Strays" was originally published in the Fall 2012 issue of *The Normal School* as "The Flipside of Mercy."

Ashland Creek Press is a small, independent publisher of books for a better planet. Our mission is to publish a range of books that foster an appreciation for worlds outside our own, for nature and the animal kingdom, for the creative process, and for the ways in which we all connect. To keep up-to-date on new and forthcoming works, subscribe to our free newsletter by visiting www.AshlandCreekPress.com.

www.ingramcontent.com/pod-product-compliance
Lightning Source LLC
Chambersburg PA
CBHW031225260626
47169CB00007B/2188